Chloe Kir

~~9 Lives~~

~~8~~

7

6

the nine lives of chloe king

The Fallen

The Stolen

The Chosen

the nine lives of chloe king

VOLUME THREE

The Chosen

by
CELIA THOMSON

SIMON PULSE
New York   London   Toronto   Sydney

First Simon Pulse edition January 2005

Copyright © 2005 by Alloy Entertainment

SIMON PULSE
An imprint of Simon & Schuster Children's Publishing Division
1230 Avenue of the Americas, New York, NY 10020

Produced by Alloy Entertainment
151 West 26th Street
New York, NY 10001

Printed in the United States of America
10 9 8 7 6 5 4 3 2 1

Library of Congress Control Number 2004112220
ISBN 0-689-86660-7

To Gg Re and Billy, love and congratulations.

One

"Hey, King, how you *feeling?*"

Chloe closed her eyes and sighed, resisting the urge to rest her head against the locker behind her. She knew Scott was just being friendly—he wasn't even making a joke—but the reality of Chloe's situation was exhausting. All her life she had been content to surf the shallow waters of the pond of high-school popularity, reveling in her basic anonymity.

Of course, all that was over now.

"I'm still a little tired," she said, turning around with a wan smile. "But mostly better. Thanks."

"Dude, that shit is *serious*. My cousin got it and he had to be homeschooled over the summer, he was so far behind." Scott adjusted his headphones and made a gunlike gesture at her. "Peace out."

Why did it have to be mono? she wondered for the fiftieth time that day. Coming down with Epstein-Barr was the fake excuse Sergei had fed the school's administrators

1

about Chloe's long absence, and even now that the dust had settled, Chloe didn't think sharing the real reason for her absence would go over too well.

Sorry about the whole not-showing-up-at-school-for-a-few-weeks thing, Chloe pictured herself saying to the principal. *You see, I'm a* cat person *and had to hide with others of my kind in a gigantic mansion called Firebird that also houses a real estate firm while this ancient Masonic-like cult tried to hunt me down because they think I killed one of their assassins. Oh, also, I have nine lives and am apparently the spiritual leader of my people, who believe they were created by ancient Egyptian goddesses.*

Nope. Chloe couldn't imagine it would fly.

"But couldn't it at least have been a brain tumor? Or even a nose job?" she wondered aloud. She watched Scott walk down the hall, slapping hands with actual friends. He was only someone that Chloe knew vaguely before, but at least his reaction was better than most. Keira Henderson, for instance, kept telling everyone how there should be a special health class devoted just to STDs and Chloe.

Of all the things Sergei had done to her, the mono/"kissing disease" lie was up there with the worst. Well, of the things she could actually *prove* he'd done, that is. It was hard to pin down exactly when keeping her safe from assassins had turned into just plain keeping her. And while the Order of the Tenth Blade was an organization whose sole purpose was to wipe out the

Mai cat people, they had kidnapped Chloe's mom, insisting it was for her own protection. At the showdown in the Presidio their leader swore that Sergei would stop at nothing to cut Chloe's ties to her human friends and families, and even though Chloe had come to see Sergei as sort of a surrogate dad over the previous few weeks, she found herself wondering if it might be true.

Chloe had really hoped life would get back to normal when she left the Mai, returned home, and went back to school. *No such luck.* Not yet, anyway. The Order was reasonably quiet now that Chloe had given up one of her lives to save her mom and everyone realized she was "the One." Plus—and Chloe wasn't even really talking to anyone at Firebird right now—her feelings toward Sergei were still unresolved, Brian was missing, and, well, she was still torn between him and Alyec. *And everyone thinks I have mono. Great.*

Chloe pulled out her cell phone and called Brian, but it clicked immediately over to voice mail, like it had the last twenty times she'd tried. And his voice mail was full. She hadn't heard anything from him since the night she'd died and come back saving her mom from the crossfire between the Mai and the Order. Brian, the *son* of the Order's leader, had come out on her side—and vengeance was promised by the rest of the Bladers. He had said his goodbyes at her window, where they'd shared a kiss through the glass pane, and then he'd disappeared into the dark city.

3

"Hey, Selina, what up?" Paul asked, going up to his own locker. He had taken to calling her that since she had told him and Amy about her true nature. Selina was Catwoman's alter ego, and, she suspected, his way of dealing with the fact that *she* had superpowers while he, the comic geek, remained a normal human. *Whatever helps him cope,* thought Chloe.

"So, besides being tired all the time and getting mocked by the general school population, are there any other symptoms of mono I should know about?" Chloe asked.

"I know you can't go to some countries in Africa because Epstein-Barr interacts with some weird fungus and can kill you," Paul said diplomatically.

"No African countries, no weird fungi. Check and check." She thought vaguely of the Pride in New Orleans, made up primarily of Mai who had chosen to stay in Africa after they were forced to leave Egypt and had eventually migrated to Louisiana.

"How you doing, dealing with being back and all?"

Chloe sighed and leaned against the lockers, hands behind her head. "Let's see. Three weeks of extratricky trig to catch up on, I somehow managed to miss the Civil War Reconstruction, and I have to figure out oxidation-reduction reactions on my own in the lab after school. Oh," she said, snapping her fingers, "*and Moby-Dick.* The entire thing, whale meat, peg legs, and all, by next Tuesday."

4

"That, uh, sucks," Paul said.

"I don't think they have invented a word beyond *sucks* yet that adequately describes my academic situation," Chloe reported. They started walking down the hall together, Chloe dragging her feet to phys ed, seriously bummed. She still hadn't decided between blowing Mr. Parmalee's mind by suddenly slam dunking something or pulling a *Smallville* and trying to hide her secret powers by acting like a normal, physically inept slacker.

"What about, you know." Paul searched for his words awkwardly, something he rarely did. He made a little clawing gesture.

"Fitting in with you monkeys like a normal human being?" Chloe said dryly. "It's really not that big a deal, Paul. I've done it my whole life."

He nodded, but Paul's expressive caterpillar eyebrows were drawn together a little, like an anime character miming worry. Paul swished down the hallway in his hipster DJ track pants and Chloe realized she hadn't seen him in khakis since . . . well, before she discovered who she really was and fell in with the Mai. As she pushed her way into the locker room, a thought occurred to her: *I wonder what else I missed.*

When she went over to Amy's that evening to study, her friend's already cloth-covered and messy bedroom looked like a costume factory had exploded—a sure sign

5

that Halloween was on its way. There were Styrofoam coffee cups filled with sequins, beads, buttons, and other shiny things dotting every free surface. Bits of lace and pieces of velvet were strewn everywhere. A glue gun and scissors and needles and a sewing machine all perched precariously in one corner, as if afraid of falling into the chaos below and being incorporated into an outfit. Amy's previous triumphs were hung on hangers, looking strangely organized against the chaos of the rest of the room. She was already playing her Halloween music: *Buffy: The Musical* blasted through her old-school wood speakers that were hidden under the craft crap.

"I'm thinking seventeenth century," Amy said, a finger to her lips. "You know, by way of the undead. Zombie, not vampire."

"Yeah. Vampires are *so* passé," Chloe muttered, erasing the math problem she was working on and starting over again. She had managed to carve herself a little nest on one end of her friend's bed and was using a bolt of muslin as a lap desk. In front of her, Chloe's notebook teetered unevenly on her math book, covered with sines and cosines and bits of equations.

Amy took her friend's comment at face value. "I *know!* Isn't it ridiculous? But this will be great. I'll use real boning in the corset this time—you know that place Dark Garden? They said they'd sell me scraps of their two-way coil boning and tips to go over them."

"Amy, I'm trying to not get held back here," Chloe said, raising her math book so she could see it. "No offense, but I really have to knuckle down."

"Oh yeah, sorry, no problem." Amy squinched her nose and Chloe tried not to laugh. Her friend's dark hair was frizzing out all around her face, exploding out of the strip of cloth she'd tried to tie it back with. There were giant, baby-diaper-sized safety pins lined up neatly on her T-shirt's shoulder, and a measuring tape hung around her neck. "I am *all* about schoolish things these days." She leapt and crash-sat on the bed, causing Chloe to hug the textbook to her chest and grab her calculator for its safety. "Look at this!"

Amy pulled a pamphlet out of the back of her jeans. She had been wearing pants a lot more often these days, ones that were—for her—surprisingly tight and shapely. *She used to, um, eschew them as being banal and pedestrian,* Chloe thought carefully, trying to use her SAT words. She took the brochure and began reading.

"*'Fit'?* What the hell is that, a new diet?"

"No, it's *F-I-T,* the Fashion Institute of Technology. In New York. It's like, the best clothing design college in the country. *Very* prestigious."

Chloe looked at the photos: people dressed weirdly— like Amy—sitting in classrooms, walking happily down the street, pinning things up on mannequins, designing jewelry on computers.

"Cool. Looks great," Chloe said, handing the pamphlet

back. "But, uh, you've got a ways to go yet, you know? We're sophomores, remember?"

"Yeah." Amy blushed and looked down. "I'm, uh, kind of thinking about graduating a year early."

"What?" Chloe demanded, putting her book aside.

"Chloe, I'm *done* here," Amy said, sighing. "I'm already taking one AP course—with just three more by next summer I'll have fulfilled all my requirements."

"I . . . shit," Chloe said, unsure what to say. The only other person she knew who'd graduated early was Halley's older brother, a certified genius who went immediately to MIT, not FIT. It wasn't the sort of thing people like *them*—her and Amy and Paul—did.

One more year and suddenly Amy would be gone from her life.

"Actually, you—I mean, what's happened with you—was a big part of my decision," Amy said shyly, her blue eyes round and big. "You know, the last month when you weren't really here, when you were doing that whole Mai thing and none of us knew what was going on—you had this whole other life going on. You're, like, a cat person, and leader of your people and dealing with feuds that go back hundreds of years and you're, like, sixteen. And still going to school. I want a cool life, too."

They were both silent for a moment.

"I'm not 'the leader of my people,'" Chloe finally mumbled, opening up her math book again.

For the next few hours they interacted normally:

Amy interrupted Chloe's studying, constantly asking what she thought of a particular fabric or lace, and Chloe responded by throwing things at her. They took a break at eight thirty and Mrs. Scotkin made them espresso and s'mores over the flames on her stove. At ten the two friends stopped working and watched *The Daily Show with John Stewart*.

On the drive home, as Amy chatted excitedly about FIT and her plans for next year, she kept looking askance at Chloe. *She's been wanting to tell me this for a while*, Chloe realized. *She's been working herself up to it.*

When they pulled up the driveway, Chloe's mom was already looking out the kitchen window for her. Amy waved. Chloe sighed and gritted her teeth. Anna King never used to do that, and if she *was* waiting up, she always made it look like she was doing something else, like watching TV or reading. Her philosophy was to respect her teenage daughter and trust her—something her ex-husband hadn't agreed with. Although Chloe hardly remembered him, her adoptive dad had had been very overprotective. He'd even told her mom that Chloe shouldn't date. Ever. Chloe wondered if it was possible that he had known who she was all along—a Mai, a lion person—and that any human she was intimate with would die.

Chloe waited as long as she could, waving at Amy until the black Malibu faded into the black night, its red taillights growing smaller like a match going out. Finally it was time to go in.

"Hey . . ." Chloe stepped inside the warm house.

"Hey, Chloe. How was your day?" Her mom sounded casual and was washing something in the sink. For just a moment, Anna King looked like a suburban housewife, not a single mom who lawyered by day and had to deal with her adopted freaky lion girl at night. Even though things had basically turned out all right, Chloe still couldn't forgive herself for her mom's kidnapping.

"All right. I got most of my math done at Amy's—if I can get through fifty pages of the *Dick* tonight, I'll be golden."

"I really wish you wouldn't call it that," Anna said, giving a smirk that was—just for a second—all lawyer and old mom. "Do you want anything to eat?"

There had suddenly been a lot of extra meat in the fridge, and while Chloe wished her mom would stop trying to be so subtly and awkwardly supportive, she was secretly grateful. She hadn't gone totally Atkins since her claws first came out, but she definitely found more of a preference for things salty and red these days.

Vampires are so passé, she thought. *Cats are in now.*

"I'll grab something in a little while. I really want to get this done." She began to head up the stairs to her room.

"Chloe?"

She stopped, cringing at the openness in her mom's voice.

"I'm really proud of you." Her mother's pixie-cut

10

hair was pulled back flat and into two tiny pigtails on the back of her head, but she still managed to look maternal and older in that instant. "Not just because of . . . everything you've been through, but how you're really working hard to get back to where you were in school. I think you're doing a great job."

"Thanks," Chloe said. She wasn't sure if she was supposed to say anything else, but her mom just nodded and went back to doing the dishes.

After the showdown at the Presidio, the two of them had had a big ol' heart-to-heart about a lot of things. Chloe told her all about her secret powers, the Mai, the Tenth Bladers who kidnapped her, how when she was dead, she saw her biological mom. Her mom had sipped scotch and listened. Finally they both cried and hugged, and that was that.

But things *had* changed between them, and she was uncomfortable even thinking about it. There was no getting around the fact that she had saved her mom's life by taking a bullet and dying, losing one of her eight remaining lives. That was a big, heavy thing for a mother to accept, a mother who still thought of herself as protector and guardian.

And Chloe didn't like the walking on eggshells her mom was doing while trying to figure out the best way to deal with her superhero teenage daughter. *I should do something bad and get grounded,* she half decided. *That would set things normal real fast.*

Her cell phone rang—or rather, Amy's cell phone, the one with the GPS that had allowed Chloe's friends to track her down when she was trying to trade herself for her mom with the Tenth Bladers, rang. Chloe hadn't given it back yet, another loose thread from the whole incident. *But not the loosest one.*

"Hey," she said, recognizing Alyec's number.

"Hello, Chloe girl! Guess where I'm calling you from?"

"The All-State after party?" she guessed.

"Absolutely! Can you believe it? There's no beer!"

"Amazing. And in our state's capital, too." Chloe smiled tiredly, dropping her books. "How was the concert?"

"Not too bad. But I'm beginning to think that the flute is for losers. I'm going to learn piccolo—at first I thought it was totally gay, but those guys get *all* of the chicks after their solos."

"Nice, Alyec."

"Hey, I gotta go, but I'll see you tomorrow, okay?"

"Yeah, see you tomorrow," Chloe said, kissing into the phone. He kissed back and she hung up.

She drew *Moby-Dick* out of her bag and leaned back on her bed, slowly turning to the page where she left off.

Okay. It's eleven fifteen. Two good hours and I'll be in the black.

But her eyes soon glazed over. The fact that it was all about the fatty part of the whale called *sperm* didn't even amuse her. She put her finger down to mark the page and looked out her window.

A round, misshapen moon rose, too white to really be called a harvest moon. Amy would be so disappointed—it wouldn't be full at Halloween but past it, already waning. Something she never would have known or noticed before becoming fully Mai. Mist or fog or smog blurred the bottom part of it and winked out the stars in the lower half of the sky.

Brian was somewhere out there. The last missing thread of the fight. All of the other key players were accounted for.

Chloe looked outside for another moment, then finally turned back to her book.

Two

She was having that dream again.

She knew it was a dream, but there was no way to stop what was about to happen: His arms had curlicues of ink and scar tissue spelling out the words *Sodalitas Gladii Decimi*. He dressed in matte black, like a shadow. His eyes were blue with something crazy in them.

Wait, there was something familiar about that. . . .

And then she ran.

She ran into an alley, even though she knew that was the wrong thing to do. In the nightmare, it was the only thing she *could* do. The darkness swallowed her whole and before she could be spat out into the other end of the alley, a barbwire-topped gate loomed above her.

His first throwing star hit her in the leg. A second caught her wrist. She fell down and he was above her, brandishing the silver dagger that would end each of her eight lives. He smiled, almost sadly, and cut her throat.

Chloe sat up in bed, covered in sweat. "*Seven* lives," she told herself aloud. "I have *seven*. That was my sister, not me."

The dreams were always about her sister, the other possible Chosen One, who had been murdered earlier that year. Once in a great while they were about her biological mother and her quest to unite all of the Eastern European Mai twenty years ago. But Chloe never had any dreams about the brother she'd been told she might have—did that mean he was still alive? Did she only relive memories of the dead at night?

Her clock radio said 4:17. It was still dark out, and the stars shone in the coldest part of the night. Chloe got up and opened the window, letting the freezing air cool her down. There was no way she was going to be able to get back to sleep anytime soon.

With one last glance toward her bed, Chloe leapt up to the sill and down onto the ground, disappearing into the darkness.

Three

"Chloe? Chloe?"

A familiar, nagging voice was . . . well, nagging her into awakeness. Chloe dizzily swam toward consciousness, suddenly aware that her left arm was asleep, crushed against the desktop.

"Maybe you really *do* have mono," Paul said, kicking her chair to rouse her. "Trig is over, buddy. The good news is that Abercrombie dashed out to make a phone call."

"Gnnerrrhh," Chloe said, trying to make her mouth work.

"What's going on with you? Burning the midnight oil? It's only a few weeks to catch up on."

"Yeah, I'm having a hard time getting a hold on this stuff. You know, like you can't train cats to do tricks? Like that. I'm a dumb cat." She stretched and, because no one was around, let her claws out. Paul still wasn't entirely used to it, and his eyes widened. *Lying to them again. What a great way to start over.*

"Yeah, that's why you're in superadvanced math. Because you're *stupid*," Paul said dryly.

Chloe shrugged, choosing not to answer. "Kim's going to help me out later with French."

"Kim can speak French?"

"Flawlessly. It's kind of eerie." Of course, watching the Mai girl with the big cat ears and slit eyes and fangs do *anything* normal was eerie, but for some reason conjugating verbs and reading aloud from *Les Liaisons Dangereuses* was particularly disturbing.

"Are you going . . . uh . . . there?" Paul asked, meaning to Firebird. She suspected that if he ever actually used the word *Mai,* he would whisper it, the way her grandmother said the word *homosexual.*

"No, I don't think so. We're going to get a cup of tea or coffee," Chloe said, shoving her notebook into her book bag and putting the pen behind her ear.

"You don't like going back there, do you?" Paul asked.

He was absolutely right. When Chloe was first taken there, it seemed like such a haven—not only were they protecting her from the Tenth Blade assassins, but Alyec, Olga, and Sergei introduced her to a whole new world. They helped find out who her biological mother was. They supported her and took her in . . .

. . . and kept her there. Everything she did, she had to do with them. She couldn't even leave by herself "for her own protection." It was only toward the end that she began to think of them as a cult.

Individual members were fine, like Alyec and Kim, one of her newest, closest friends. And Igor and Valerie were harmless, even if they bought into the whole philosophy of the place.

It was Sergei she didn't want to think about.

There was no *proof* that he'd sent members of the Mai's warrior class, the kizekh, to kill her mom. On Chloe's one real escape from Firebird, while they were "protecting" her from the Tenth Blade, Amy and Paul had told her that they thought something weird was going on at her house—like that her mom was never there anymore. As soon as Chloe realized her mom had been kidnapped, Kim had volunteered her particularly feline talents to search Chloe's house for clues. The girl with the cat ears had not only sniffed out traces of humans from the Order—but also the presence of Mai. What had they been doing there? If it was just to watch and protect her mom, surely Sergei would have told her . . . wouldn't he?

Kim had darkly hinted that Chloe wasn't the first Mai raised by humans whose human parents had "disappeared" in order for the orphan to be brought back into the fold. But even if Sergei hadn't been planning to actually kill her mom, he also refused to rescue her from the Tenth Bladers. When Chloe finally decided to "fix" everything by offering to trade herself for her mom, both sides showed up at the Presidio—along with Kim, Alyec, Paul, and Brian—for a royal showdown that ended in Chloe losing one of her lives.

Sergei had let out a shot, but Chloe still wasn't sure who the bullet had been meant for. Had it been really aimed at Brian and not her mom? Could it have been meant for Chloe? Sergei had taken her in and treated her like a daughter, lecturing her, playing chess with her, eating dinner with her, and doing other dad things that she had never gotten from her real father *or* the adopted one who took off when she was little. And there was the whole being-the-One thing she didn't want to deal with, either. It would effectively mean usurping Sergei's leadership of the Mai, which wasn't something Chloe particularly wanted to do or even talk about.

"Yeah, I'm a little off the whole kitty-kennel thing right now," she admitted.

"I don't blame you. Hey, did I tell you I'm going to audition to spin at the fall formal?" He held up some twelve-inch records and waved them excitedly.

"You're going to make them dig up a turntable?" Chloe asked dryly. They started toward *The Lantern*'s office, the school newspaper Paul sort-of worked on so he could get access to their office and computers.

"What? No. They're totally not that hip. I just bought these off of Justin. I'm using my iPod and a computer."

"Wow. That's *so* old school."

"Piss off, King. At least we'll get to hear some good stuff this year."

"Yes, but can we dance to it?"

"I'm *counting* on you to help fill the floor until things

20

pick up," Paul said earnestly. "I even promised Amy and some of her gothier friends that I'd play some Switchblade Symphony and New Order in the first set."

"You know, you should actually write something for the paper sometime," Chloe said as Paul unlocked the office door to *The Lantern*'s office. She didn't actually work on the school newspaper herself but often took advantage of the couch and computers that her friend had access to because of his position as editor. "Put your vast musical knowledge to use. Write a 'just released' column or something. Get some college application points."

"Huh." He paused, considering it. "Sure would beat editing the crappy freshman editorials. Well, that's why you're the brains of the operation."

"Nah, just the brawn. *And* the claws." Chloe shuffled in after he opened the door for her, prepared to throw her backpack onto the couch like she always did before throwing herself onto it, but she stopped herself midswing, just in time to keep from throwing the ten-pound bag onto Amy's head. She was flipping through a copy of *The Nation*, her legs primly crossed, pretending not to have realized she'd surprised Chloe and Paul.

"Hey, guys," Amy said casually. "What's up?"

"Not much—how'd you get in here?" Paul didn't sound as thrilled as he probably should have been—his girlfriend had decided to surprise him by suddenly appearing in a semiprivate room. Once Chloe left, it would probably mean a major snogging session—what gave?

"Carson let me in." Amy jerked her thumb over her shoulder. Somewhere in the supplies closet, someone was rummaging.

"I can take off . . . ," Chloe suggested. She would have to find someplace else to nap—maybe under the bleachers at gym? The only people to find her would be janitors or dealers, and neither would show up until after school.

"Nah, it's okay," Amy said, putting the magazine down.

"Good." Chloe heaved a sigh of relief and fell down next to Amy, immediately curling up and putting her head on one of the well-worn and slightly grimy pillows.

Carson came out of the supply closet and glared at the three of them. "Paul, you're an editor. You *work* here—you can't just keep using this place as your private club room."

"Actually, I'm a columnist now," Paul said with an evil grin.

"I've got an idea," Chloe called sleepily from the couch. "You shut up about us being here, and we won't tell Keira that you made the hot and heavy with Halley last night."

Carson didn't even try to deny it; he just huffed and spun on his heel back into the supply closet.

"And *how* do we know that?" Amy asked, looking at Chloe.

Paul pointed at his nose and made a little cat-clawing motion with his hand.

"Oh, right. Nice work, Chlo."

But Chloe was already fast asleep.

Alyec actually took her out to dinner that evening—a diner, but at least it wasn't McDonald's—and gossiped about the band trip. He was as bad as a girl, his eyes lighting up delightedly as he related the exploits and disasters of various hookups that had occurred. No wonder he didn't mind the cultish aspects of Firebird: it was just one big soap opera to him.

The lighting in the diner was dismally fluorescent and the decor was faded plastic aqua, all the way from the scratched-up bar to the bench seat Chloe's ass was sticking to. Outside giant pane windows, the blackness was solid except for the lights of an occasional passing bus—kind of like that famous painting by Edward Hopper. It was a far cry from Firebird, with its velvet curtains and mahogany desks.

It was the same place where Alyec, Kim, Paul, and Amy had eaten after the fight at the Presidio, wondering what was going to happen next. Chloe had gone home with her mom and had the big talk about everything she had been hiding for the past couple of months: the claws, the Mai, *everything*. Afterward Brian had said goodbye to Chloe through her bedroom window.

She probably shouldn't have been thinking about

him while she was at dinner with Alyec, but it was hard not to. She nodded when it seemed appropriate and grunted at regular intervals.

". . . and then I shot flaming chickens out of my ass," Alyec finished, biting off the end of a fry that was speared on his fork.

"Uh, what? Sorry," Chloe said when she realized exactly what he had said.

"You're not listening! They're talking about actually having a *king* and *queen* of the formal—like out of some cheesy old movie or something."

"Oh. Bizarre." She stared out the window, looking at the darkness, concentrating on not letting her eyes go slitty. She could feel the muscles tensing.

"Is there something you want to talk about, Chloe King?" He mock-frowned when he said it, but Chloe could see the worry in his eyes.

This was her chance to be honest, to let him know how confused she was about him and Brian, even though Brian was nowhere to be found.

Nope. Not yet. She just couldn't.

"Remember when we were eating Chinese," she said instead, "and you told me that it was hard for you sometimes to relate to normal humans and normal human life?"

"Yes. We had chicken and ten-vegetable lo mein," he recalled fondly.

"How do you do it?" Chloe asked earnestly.

He raised his eyebrows, surprised by the directness of her question.

"I don't know. . . ." He squirmed uncomfortably, like a completely normal human teenage male. A lock of thick blond hair fell into his eyes. "I have fun with everyone at school, but I'm not really that *close* to them, you know. They think it's because I'm Russian or supercool or something. And . . ." He frowned, thinking about it. "And I've got my mom, and my dad when he bothers to come home, and everyone else—I grew up Mai, you know? Surrounded by them. It's easy to be 'normal' in the day if you can relax with others like you at night."

"Oh. Right," Chloe said glumly, picturing her own mother and house in the evening. Not exactly relaxing. She suspected that if there was a book called *Dealing with Your Adopted Mai Child,* her mom would have already read it and decided to make sure Chloe was appreciating her native culture. *Difficult when my ethnicity is a big ol' secret and my people can—and do—take down running deer with their bare claws.*

"And . . . you're *different,* Chloe," he continued gently. "Even from us. You're our spiritual leader—you have nine lives. Chloe, you *died* and came back to life. *Twice.* That makes you different from *everyone.* "

Chloe began to suck noisily on her chocolate milk shake, not wanting to hear about it. There were big issues—death, the afterlife, the goddesses of the Mai, God in general—concepts of thousands of years and infinities, and she wasn't really prepared to think about them right now. Maybe never. Dying and coming back to life *was* weird. And she didn't want it to have anything to do with her current ennui at school.

"I'm sorry," Alyec said instantly, seeing her look. He brushed her cheek with his hand. "We don't have to talk about this. But you asked. I think maybe readjusting to your old life is going to be . . . difficult, Chloe."

"*So* not the answer I wanted," she growled.

"Okay, how about this: If you have sex with me—like actual sex—I promise it will fix everything. Including your acne."

Chloe cracked up. *That* was what she needed right now—to laugh, even if it only put off thinking about the inevitable for a little while.

"Wait," she said, suddenly sobering. "What acne?"

Four

"*Il faut que* *nous parlous*," Kim repeated patiently.

"*Il faut que nous parlous*," Chloe said, trying to copy the sounds exactly.

"Better. Now can you give me *all* of the present subjunctive of *parler?*"

They sat on the roof of Café Eland, Chloe with a latte and Kim with her green tea. While the other Mai girl was growing more and more curious about Chloe's daily life in San Francisco proper and what "normal" teenagers did, she was still too shy to ask. It had taken a *lot* of pleading from Chloe—as well as personal coaching on how the buses and BART worked—to get Kim to agree to meet in the city instead of at Firebird.

"*Parle, parles, parle, parlous, parliez, parlient . . .*"

"*Parlent*," Kim corrected. Then one of her ears flicked back and for just a moment her eyes narrowed. "Your friends are here—in the café below us. They just came in."

"Amy and Paul? I'm not meeting them tonight," Chloe said, intrigued. And willing to do almost anything other than conjugate verbs.

"Perhaps they're on a date," Kim said mildly.

"Maybe." Chloe crawled over to the heating vent and put her ear up next to it. Her hearing was nowhere near as good as Kim's, but it was still several times better than a normal human's. It took her a moment to sort through the extraneous noise: chairs scraping against the floor, the cash register ringing, other people talking, before she was able to single out her friends.

"Yeah, she kind of freaked when I told her." That was Amy, settling herself into one of the big, comfy chairs. Chloe could imagine her friend tucking her long legs up underneath her, looking like a little girl in a big chair. *Affected, but cute.*

"Well, it's big news." That was Paul, stirring even more sugar into his hot chocolate.

"*You* didn't freak out."

"I want whatever's best for you." There was a pause and some wooden-sounding noises, like someone was pushing around them to get by.

"You up to a long-distance relationship?" Amy said this perkily, but there was something in her voice, something strained. Something *testing*—like this was a question on which many other things were balanced.

Paul let out a sigh, which he tried to cover by blowing on his drink.

"Amy, I'm not sure we're up to a *close-distance* relationship," he finally said.

There was a long, frosty pause. Even Chloe stopped breathing.

"What's that supposed to mean?"

"I . . . We . . . It hasn't been . . . You haven't felt anything weird recently?"

"Well, yeah." Amy probably had that angry-sarcastic look on her face, where she scrunched up her nose. "What with saving Chloe and the cat-people thingy and Halloween coming up and all . . . What are you *saying*, Paul Chun?"

"I don't know. With Chloe back, it's kind of like the old days. Maybe this—*us*—is just sort of an aberration. A *nice* one," he added quickly. "But maybe we were trying to make too big a thing out of some sexual tension and all the other weird things going on."

"It's *not* the old days, dipshit," Amy snapped. Usually she used that word endearingly, but there was very little warmth in her voice this time. "Chloe's a freaking *cat person*. Who lived with other *cat people*. Who are hunted by other *crazy people*."

Chloe's stomach sank into a little ball. Amy wasn't actually saying anything *bad* about her, but hearing about herself and her recent life put that way was . . . cold. Kim looked away, pretending not to have heard.

"And if there's a problem between us, it's between *us*," Amy went on to say. "Leave Chloe out of it."

29

There was another moment's silence that must have been horribly awkward between her two friends. When Amy spoke again, there were tears in her voice.

"I—*I've* been pretty happy recently," she said weakly, talking in quick sips, the way you do when you're trying not to cry. "I know I've been busy. . . . What's *wrong?*"

Chloe moved her head away from the vent, not wanting to hear any more. She felt a little disgusted with herself for having heard that much. If it had been anyone else in the world or just *one* of her friends with someone else, she wouldn't have minded at all. She probably would have kept listening. But this was way, *way* too close.

"They're breaking up," she said tonelessly, crawling back over to Kim. "Or Paul's dumping her, I guess."

Kim didn't say anything, just watched her with large, unblinking green cat eyes.

"I should have realized something was going on," Chloe continued. "I should have noticed—they haven't been spending as much time together lately, and Paul doesn't seem to want her around much."

"What was her big news?" Kim asked, then suddenly remembered she had been pretending not to listen. She looked around herself uncertainly but didn't blush. *Just like a cat,* Chloe thought, smiling inside a little.

"She's graduating from high school a year early. It *did* freak me out." She sighed. "She never talked about this before—I don't know, it was just kind of sudden."

"It seems that the three of you are each beginning to head down very different paths," Kim said slowly.

"I hope you're not going to start talking to me about this whole being-the-One crap again," Chloe said, more harshly than she meant.

Kim lowered her eyes back to the French textbook. "I meant exactly what I said. But you *will* find it more difficult to escape your . . . heritage than you think." Chloe was glad that she hadn't used the word *destiny*, but she still didn't like it.

"I'm sick of people telling me that!" Chloe stood up. "I am *sixteen*. I have spent my *entire life* as a 'normal human.' It can't all suddenly change. I want to get good grades, go out and party, go to the dance, go to college. Which is hard enough with the weeks I lost! I don't have time for this, or Amy and Paul suddenly calling it quits, or my mom acting all weird around me. . . ."

"You want to go back to the old days."

"Yes, I . . . Shut up."

"What do you intend to do after we finish here?" Kim asked her.

That threw Chloe off. "What?"

"When we finish your French lesson here, what will you do?"

"I'm going to, uh . . ." *Go home, read some, and go to sleep.* These words had been well prepared, rehearsed, and used many times since she had returned from Firebird. But she couldn't lie into Kim's big cat eyes.

31

Chloe thought about what Amy had said about her and wondered if she was actually fooling anyone. "Go running," she finished lamely, sure that Kim would know what she meant.

Kim leaned over and, in a rare move, actually *touched* Chloe, wrapping her hand with her clawed paw.

"Whatever you decide to do," she said levelly, "don't lie to *yourself*, Chloe."

Chloe thought about Kim's words as she raced across the skyline, leaping and tumbling over rooftops and electric poles. She couldn't ignore the fact that she was cheating by coming out here at night, that she was stealing time from schoolwork and lying to people. Before—weeks ago—she had been able to ignore all that and just enjoy the freedom of the night. And now she couldn't.

Chloe.

She stopped suddenly. There was a whisper, an almost-voice that sounded like it was calling her name. The wind had picked up and was whistling through the old dead antennas that still decorated some rooftops like cactus spines. Chloe put her nose to the air and turned her head, trying to focus her ears on the sound.

"Mirao."

Without thinking, she turned and followed the sound, leaping across a gap to the roof of the house beyond. There, sitting primly in front of the round chimney of an oil furnace, was a little black cat. Its whiskers and chest were white, matched by little white socks. A *dairy* cat, her mom would have called him. The kind that hung around dairy barns, catching rats and in return being given bowls of fresh milk.

What's it doing up here? Chloe wondered. As she looked around for a door or skylight that was left open, the cat demurely picked up a paw and began licking it, like it had all the time in the world. Like it wasn't a little tiny cat on a cold rooftop in a big city with winter coming on.

"Hey, little guy." Chloe figured that being Mai, she should be able to speak cat or something—but apparently not. It paused, its licking for a moment, then went back to work.

"You shouldn't be up here. Are you lost?"

Chloe crept closer to it, making the *tchk tchk* noises that Amy's cat always came running to. She crouched down and started to extend her hand, but the little cat leapt up to the top of the chimney, out of her reach.

"Mirao!" it said again, louder.

"Come on, easy now." Chloe dug her toe claws into the brick and prepared to push herself up. "You might be able to outrun a normal human, but I'm afraid—" She swiped her hand up, but the little cat jumped down and ran faster than Chloe's claws could come out, scrabbling its feet like a cartoon. "Kitty!" Chloe called, beginning to get annoyed.

She ran across the roof after it, but it leapt over the side of the building.

"No!" Chloe looked down to the street. She couldn't see into the darkness below, even with her cat eyesight.

"Mirao!"

Chloe looked up: the cat was on the roof of the far building, patiently waiting for her. It must have dived down to a window ledge and then climbed back up again. "Mir-ao!"

"I get it now. You want to play, is that it? We're playing tag?" It wasn't a lost little kitty—it was an alley cat, or a *sky cat,* more like. This was its world, and it just wanted to play with a newcomer. "Okay!"

Chloe grinned and leapt. The cat waited a moment, as if giving her a fair start, then took off—pausing now and then to make sure she was following.

This is great. I should totally get a cat, Chloe decided. And it wasn't as if her mom could really object to having one in the house anymore.

Whenever she got too close, Chloe made herself slow down; neither she nor her playmate wanted the game to end too soon. She smiled, wondering what they might look like to a random bystander: a witch and her familiar flying across the upper stories of the city? A large cat hunting a smaller one? *Maybe they would just dismiss it.* Halloween was just around the corner; anything supernatural seemed possible.

Suddenly the dairy cat veered to the left, down to the top of a fire escape.

"Ha! Getting tired?" Chloe taunted.

The cat gave her what she could have sworn was a nasty look.

"Okay, but I can't play too much on the streets with you," she warned. "I can't let other people see me."

"Mirao!" The cat turned and slipped down the metal stairs like a black Slinky.

"Is this your home? Are you showing me your—?" Suddenly Chloe stopped, forgetting the cat entirely. The fire escape led down into a dark dead-end alley, apparently unused except for garbage collection. Most of the pavement was pocked and puddled with slick black flats of shiny city water.

There was an ominous outline that cut into the oily reflections, large and organic and shaped suspiciously like a body.

And there was a smell . . . a familiar smell . . .

Chloe leapt straight down the last two floors, landing in a crouch just inches away from the edge of the shape. She crawled over closer and as her eyes adjusted saw what was indeed a human body, unmoving and broken looking.

It was Brian.

Five

"Oh my God—"

Chloe put a hand to his neck, carefully retracting her claws. There was a pulse—but it was sluggish. His skin was cold and clammy, as if his body could no longer fight the chilly environment around him.

"Chloe?" Brian croaked.

Chloe ran her hands over his body, trying to see and feel what was wrong. He moaned and struggled a little—it didn't look like his neck or back were broken.

He held his hands over the top of his stomach, just under his chest. When Chloe pushed them aside, warm, syrupy blood seeped out. His entire shirt was soaked, and slow rivers of it ran down his sides and congealed in the water. A knife wound. Of course it was a knife wound. While the Order of the Tenth Blade used nine daggers to kill all nine lives of a Pride Leader, it took only one dagger to kill a member of the Order who betrayed them.

"You were supposed to run away—to disappear!" Chloe cried, trying not to panic.

Brian tried to say something, but nothing came out. He took a deep breath and opened his eyes. For a moment he saw her clearly—or at least the shape of her, since it was too dark for human vision—and smiled. Then he passed out again.

"Fuck," Chloe swore. Where could she take him? If she brought him to a public hospital, he'd be a sitting duck for the Order to finish the job. She couldn't protect him twenty-four/seven and had no idea how to go about hiring a bodyguard—especially one that didn't work for Brian's dad's security company.

There was home, where she had taken Alyec after Brian wounded *him* by the bridge. But as much as that thought appealed to her, Chloe had made a firm decision not to put her mom at risk again with her strange life. The Tenth Blade had already broken into their home once to kidnap Chloe's mom; bringing a man there they wanted dead was just asking for trouble. Which left only one option: the Firebird mansion. The home base of the Mai.

"Holy ironic justice, Batman," she muttered as she knelt down to gather Brian up in her arms.

Once again the similarities between Chloe and a real superhero ended when she realized that carrying him all the way to Sausalito would not only be impractical, it would be really slow. And there was no way she was going to be able to get a cab that would be willing to pick up a girl with her bloody, injured boyfriend. Of course, the bus was out, too.

She resorted to the only superweapon she had: her cell phone. She punched the numbers quickly. Alyec had a car, but only when he stole it. Which left . . .

"'Sup?" Amy's cheery voice came over the other end.

"Amy, I need you—it's an emergency. I found Brian—bleeding to death in an alley. I need to get him help."

"Ohmygod. Where are you?"

"Somewhere near Chinatown." She looked around, but the alley had no name. "Track me on your phone." Amy had the other matching GPS cell phone so they could track each other; the only downside was that its screen wasn't very big, and Amy had to look at it while driving.

"I'll be there ASAP."

With the little bubble of normal conversation over, Chloe became more aware of the loneliness of the alley and the silence of Brian. She couldn't remember much of junior high first aid and hoped she was doing the right thing by tearing off the sleeves of her shirt and tying them around his wound. Apart from that and trying to keep him from rolling through the puddles—though even the dry part of the cobblestone lane wasn't a particularly sterile environment—there was little Chloe could do besides comfort him and wait.

"What's going on here?"

Chloe turned to look at the owner of the new voice. A pair of boys, too healthy to be street people, too confident to be scared of a lonely alley. Both were muscled. Asian. All in black . . . *gang* members.

"You got a problem?" the other asked, smiling. Take away the attitude and the tattoos and it was obvious they were barely twenty. And actually pretty good-looking.

This could go two ways, Chloe realized. One of which was that they could turn out to be reasonably decent local guys who just wanted to help. But Chloe wasn't going to wait around to see if it was the other—more likely—possibility.

With a frightful hiss she leapt up, extending her hand and foot claws, making sure her slit eyes flashed in the light. In two springs she was a foot from them, yowling and swiping her claws.

"Li Shou!" one of them cried. Then they turned around and fled.

"Almost too easy," Chloe murmured. She retracted her claws and walked back to Brian, who suddenly looked a little too still. She knelt beside him and began stroking his hair. "Stay awake—you've got to stay awake. . . ."

He groaned in response, but his mouth was moving like he was trying to say something.

"Leave me," he whispered. *"They'll be back. It's over. . . ."*

"Not on your life, sweetie," she said with a forced grin. "Help's on the way."

"Chloe . . ." His lips moved more, but nothing came

out. Chloe leaned closer. Then he fell back, unconscious.

"Brian, no," she whispered, her eyes filling with tears.

Ten minutes later Amy arrived in her brother's old black station wagon. Chloe took most of Brian's weight because of her superior strength but needed Amy to hold him straight and steady in case there *was* actually something wrong with his back.

"Holy shit," was all her friend said. They carefully laid him down in the backseat and, completely unconscious, he didn't even groan. His skin was deathly white.

"Sorry," Chloe said, taking the driver's seat. "The hideout's kind of a secret, and you're going to have to blindfold yourself somehow. . . ."

Amy looked a little piqued, but only for an instant. "No problem. As the loyal sidekick, I should expect to be put into ridiculous situations." She leapt into shotgun and pulled a jacket over her head.

Chloe burned rubber pulling out, and as she turned onto the street, a man-shaped shadow hugged the wall near the entrance to the alley, watching the car go. But *one* person couldn't have done this to Brian. . . . It looked like he had been beaten from all sides at once. And it wasn't like the Tenth Blade to skulk in the shadows: if they knew a Mai was there, they would have come out and tried to kill Chloe, too.

She didn't begin breathing normally until they were going over the bridge, shooting past the National

Guard, who had been on her ass after the big duke-out with the Rogue.

Ignoring the niceties of *road* and *right-of-way,* Chloe took the car off road the moment they turned onto the street that led to Firebird.

"My brother's going to *kill me* . . . ," Amy muttered from under the jacket.

Chloe drove around to the back of the estate and honked the horn, shouting, "It's me!" as she barreled up to the gate, which the guard opened just in time for the car *not* to crash into it. On the old TV show the Batmobile came roaring through a discreetly hidden tunnel into Wayne Manor; Batman didn't need Alfred to let him in.

Must do something about that.

She pulled up to the kitchen, or back entrance, door and jumped out. By the time she had jumped out, someone was already opening the door, curious about the late-night intrusion. When she saw who it was, the female Mai bowed her head. "You have come back, Leader."

"I need to get him into a bed or something," Chloe ordered. "*Help* me."

The woman opened her eyes and sniffed the air. "But he—and she—are *human!*"

"Can I take this off yet?" Amy asked, still in the front seat under the jacket.

"Please! I'm begging you!" Chloe cried, frustrated.

42

"The One doesn't need to beg," the woman murmured. She called behind her in either Russian or Mai; Chloe wasn't listening enough to be able to tell the difference.

That's Eleni, Chloe thought distractedly as the woman hurried back over to the car to help her with Brian. Eleni was one of the Mai who had most recently come from Turkey, like Chloe's biological family. "Just two more minutes," Chloe told Amy.

Among the other Mai who showed up—some bleary-eyed, some wide awake—was Ellen, the kizekh who used to be Chloe's sort-of bodyguard when she had lived with them full-time, just a short time ago. Her partner, Dmitry, wasn't with her, which was unusual. She grinned at Chloe before giving a slight bow, genuinely glad to see her back. Everyone else bowed deeply and politely eased Chloe out of the way while carrying Brian in.

"Where are you taking him?" Chloe asked.

"The emergency ward, Honored One." Ellen winked. "Don't worry—we'll have him fixed up good as new." The Mai disappeared down the halls of the house at a trot.

"Emergency ward? We have an *emergency* ward?" Chloe wondered as she took Amy by the hand and followed them. *There really is a whole little world inside these walls.*

This was obviously one of the oldest parts of the mansion. She hadn't been here before and was struck by the narrow stone hallways and cold, damp smell—like there was a well or a cellar nearby. Something caught inside

Chloe: this was an old house, like right out of something on PBS, and she had full non-museum-pass access. She could even *live* here if she wanted.

They wound up in a dark room whose lights came on a second after they got there, switched by a female Mai rubbing her eyes and pulling on a white lab coat. There were two hospital-style beds, what looked suspiciously like a gleaming, stainless-steel operating table in the middle of the floor, and antique metal cabinets full of medical equipment. The floor was old wood, completely clashing with the sterile nature of everything else.

Ellen and the other Mai carrying Brian carefully put him on the operating table.

"A *human?*" The doctor was a tiny woman with a body like Tinkerbell and huge, dark hazel—almost brown—eyes, a color unusual among the Mai. She was probably in her late thirties, but it was hard to tell.

Ellen quietly jerked her head at Chloe.

"*Oh.*" She bowed her head and spread her hands, palms up, a curt but heartfelt gesture of respect. Then she immediately began examining Brian, who made pathetic little sounds as she prodded him.

"Why does the other human have a jacket over her head?" Ellen whispered to Chloe.

"I was trying to keep the location of Firebird secret," Chloe whispered back, not wanting to tear her eyes from Brian. The doctor was ripping off Chloe's make-do bandages and probing the wound. Instead of normal medical instruments she used her claws, with amazing precision.

"Someone clean this guy up with sterile towels while I work on him," the doctor snapped. "The rest of you"—she looked up, managing to fix everyone with the same look—"*get out!*"

"Please, Honored One," she added to Chloe after a moment.

Chloe paced in the small study outside that served as a waiting room. Everyone else went to bed, bowing obeisances and backing away from her just like she had seen them do with Sergei. The gestures seemed a little more extreme, a little more heartfelt than the ones for him, though. Ellen had brought the back of Chloe's hand to her forehead as she bowed, like something a knight would do in the Dark Ages, swearing fealty. It was all a little uncomfortable.

Chloe had expected many things if she ever returned to the mansion or the Mai: disappointment about Chloe's decision to leave them, anger over Chloe's love for humans, sadness that they had "lost" someone to the outside world. Cold shoulders, at least. And maybe, from the slicker ones who wanted her back in the fold, hugs and kisses and smothering love. But certainly not worship.

It looks like they would do anything for me, she mused distractedly. Their immediate agreement to help Brian was unbelievable. Not only was he a human, not only was he once a member of the Tenth Blade, but he was the *son* of the *head* of the Order. The enemy was in their camp and they'd welcomed him with open arms. Well, sort of.

"So wait, what was that you were saying before? That I'm the hero and you're my *sidekick?*" she finally asked, trying to distract herself with her and Amy's previous conversation in the car.

"Yeah, like Batman and Robin. Xena and Gabrielle," came the voice under the jacket.

"Um, we're not gay. At least not me. And what about Paul? Who's he?"

Silence.

"Arch-villain, maybe," Amy countered. "Nemesis, perhaps. He's already jealous of your powers. Right now he could be plotting your doom."

"You, uh, you want to talk about something?" Chloe ventured. It was a strange way to have this conversation: while she was nervous about Brian, at Firebird, with her friend, who had a jacket over her head. Yet it seemed as good a time as any.

There was a pause. "No," Amy said stubbornly, but she didn't sound certain.

"I heard you and Paul talking at the coffee shop earlier. I wasn't spying on you," Chloe added quickly, reacting to the face she knew her friend was making. "I was practicing verb forms with Kim on the roof."

"He wants to break up," Amy said softly.

"And you . . . ?"

"I thought it was pretty good. . . . I mean, it wasn't perfect—he's a little hard to get through to sometimes. But it's a *real* relationship. Not like any of the other guys I dated . . . We were doing it right. Friends *first,* you know?"

"Yeah, but . . ." Chloe bit her lip, unsure how to say it. "Philosophy aside, do you *like* him?"

"Yes," Amy said, a catch in her throat. "When he isn't being a *douche bag!*"

"Did he start acting like this before or after you told him about graduating a year early?"

"Why?" her friend demanded.

"Well . . . it's a big thing, Amy. Kind of out of the blue." Chloe realized she was no longer talking about Paul. "I mean, it wasn't like you were planning it all along. . . ."

"Well, your *turning into a cat* kind of came out of nowhere, too!" Amy snapped indignantly.

Chloe took a deep breath, forcing herself not to respond to that. It was hard.

"Yeah, but you're going to be leaving us. Permanently—the beginning of the end, you know? It's hard for me to imagine losing you. And I'll bet it's harder for Paul, who's in the middle of losing his family. His parents have barely spoken since the divorce began."

Amy grew silent and seemed to pull into herself a little, as if she was actually thinking about this.

Just then Kim came calmly padding into the room. "Hello, Chloe. Hello, Amy." Once again, the girl with the giant cat ears was unfazed by anything; it was like she had been expecting them.

"Hi, Kim," said Amy from underneath the jacket, like Cousin It.

"I think you can take off the blindfold now, if that's what that is." Kim didn't smile, but Chloe was beginning to get used to the other girl's extremely dry sense of humor.

She pulled Amy's jacket off as gently as possible. Her friend's frizzy hair staticked anyway, billowing around her head like a goth clown's.

"How'd you know it was me?" Amy asked, running her hands back over her hair, trying to do something with it and failing.

"Your smell," Kim answered primly.

"Yeah?" Amy wrinkled her nose, also sniffing. "Speaking of, it *definitely* smells a lot like cat here. . . ."

Kim looked startled and slightly mortified.

"So this is the Cat Cave, huh? The secret hideout?" Amy looked around eagerly.

"I'll give you the tour later," Chloe promised.

"What happened?" Kim asked.

"I found Brian left half dead on the street. I think the Tenth Blade probably thought they finished him off, or maybe some people came by and interrupted their 'business. . . .'"

"And you brought him here." It was a statement, a wry question, an accusation, all in one.

"What else was I supposed to do?" Chloe demanded. "I know it's weird and I'm sorry—I could promise it will never happen again, but I don't think I can promise anything anymore. I'll make it up somehow. . . ." She sat on the couch, head in her hands. "No one really seemed to mind that much," she added, to the floor.

"That is because you are the One, Chloe," Kim said gently, sinking gracefully onto the couch next to her. Amy took a plush chair across from them. "They would die for you if you commanded it."

"That's ridiculous," Chloe muttered.

"It's the truth. I know this is hard, but you are our spiritual leader. You always have been. It's not so much your destiny as your birthright."

"But some of these people are too young to have ever even had a . . . uh, *the One* before! Why should they just suddenly accept me as their new leader?"

"Chloe, *the One* is not an inherited position, like a king or certain Republican presidents," Kim said with the faintest smile and Chloe got her joke. "Just because someone is Kemnet'r doesn't mean that his or her child will be. The One must be *different:* not only pure of heart, strong, determined, and willing to do good, but chosen and blessed by the Twin Goddesses with the abilities to make things so. Nine lives, to lead her people to battle again and again if need be. *Connection* with the past, previous Chosen Ones. Connection with the present, her Pride, in a way that is beyond metaphysical."

Chloe looked at her.

"I don't know about the last two." Then she remembered a presence at death, a feeling of her mother being there. Comforting like a powerful protector, powerful as anything that could defeat death. "Okay, just the last one."

"You stopped a battle between your Pride and the Tenth Blade single-handedly," Amy pointed out.

"I *died*, remember? *That's* what put the kibosh on things."

"Even so," Kim said, nodding.

Chloe sat back, feeling somehow defeated in the face of the eternally calm—and serene—girl next to her. "*You* don't worship me, though, right?" she said in a small voice. "You're, like, my only real friend here."

Kim cocked her head, thinking about it for a moment. "I . . . revere the position of the One and her sacred duties," she said slowly. "And no leader is ever perfect, even ones gifted with the divine. You, like every Kemnet'r before you—you could definitely use an adviser."

"Hey," Chloe said, annoyed but amused. "I said *friend*, not adviser."

Kim turned her paws up, shrugging, but there was a wry smile on her lips. "I think you may find you need both in the upcoming days."

"I'll be the friend," Amy said diplomatically. "You can be the adviser."

"I never said I was going to take this on," Chloe

pointed out. "I'm from a culture of choices, you know. Not destinies."

"As the old man said in that movie you took me to, 'You must of course do what you think is right,'" Kim said, referring to the night they had all gone to see *Star Wars*. "But whatever choice you make as the One, it can only *be* right."

"No pressure, though," Chloe muttered sarcastically. First Amy offered to be Jet Girl to her Tank; now Kim wanted to be Obi-Wan to her Luke. It was kind of bizarre.

The door to the emergency room opened and the doctor came out with her hands shoved deep in her pockets, just like on TV. She even bowed that way. Even though being bowed to all the time was weird, it *was* pretty good for the ego. Like the cute waiters at a Japanese restaurant. *Of course, I'll have to put a stop to it.*

"Okay, your friend is pretty badly banged up. Not only has he lost a lot of blood, but there's an injury to the back of his head that looks serious. His right arm is broken, five of his ribs are cracked, his left leg is broken, and some of his toes have been crushed."

She waited a moment, a questioning look in her eye. Chloe didn't say anything, unsure what she wanted.

"Can I ask . . . ?" the doctor finally prompted.

"He sort of quit the Tenth Blade, something I guess you just don't do. And he did it when we were all duking it out at the Presidio, trying to save me and my mom from the Bladers when he should have been fighting *with* them. So they made him number one on their hit list. Even though he's like Order of the Tenth Blade royalty or something," she added.

"*That's* Brian Rezza? Son of Whitney, the head of the Order?" The doctor gave a low whistle. "And his own people did this to him?"

"They are obviously not his people anymore," Kim said dryly.

"And they call *us* feral." She sighed. "I'm going to be honest with you: I don't know the extent of the damage to the head yet and if he *does* recover, it's going to be a long, painful process. You don't know his blood type, do you? Regardless, someone will need to get a couple of quarts of it."

As hard as she tried to stop it, Chloe's eyes filled with tears. *Real leaders don't cry so easy.* Just more proof of her point.

"I'll fix what I can here, but if you don't want to take him to a real hospital, a lot of his healing is going to depend on his own body." She ran a hand, claws now safely sheathed, through her shoulder-length brown hair. "We've never been introduced, I don't think. I'm Doctor Calie Lovsky." She put out her hand and Chloe extended hers, thinking that they were going to do that special "secret" Mai handshake Igor had taught her: slight extension of the claws to graze the other's palm. Instead, like Ellen, she took the back of Chloe's hand and put it on her forehead. Unlike Ellen, she didn't bow.

"Is, uh, everyone going to keep doing this?" Chloe asked, turning to Kim.

"The kizekh will. For everyone else, it's only the first time they are formally introduced to you."

"I'm so glad you're here," Dr. Lovsky said, putting her hands back in her pockets. "We really need you."

Her easy switch from doctor to worshipful servant gave Chloe emotional whiplash. The woman was older than she, *waaaay* better educated, and a doctor besides. *What the hell is she doing looking up to* me?

"Can I go see him?" she finally asked.

"Yeah, but as the old platitude goes, don't stay too long; he needs his rest."

Chloe started to walk past her into the room, then stopped. "I'm—I'm really sorry about bringing a human here."

"Whatever the One wills," the doctor said, shrugging.

They had moved Brian to a bed and replaced his clothes with a simple cotton hospital tunic. He had also been bathed; most of the dried and sticky blood was gone. As were two of his teeth, Chloe noted with a shiver of horror. Like someone had kicked him in the mouth when he was down. There was a white bandage around his head and another around his chest. A clean white sheet was pulled up to his neck.

"Hey," Chloe said softly. "How you doing?"

A disturbing gurgle came from the back of Brian's throat. He coughed a couple of times, trying to clear the blood out, but then winced because of the pain in his chest. His crusted eyes flicked halfway open. When he saw her, he smiled. Chloe touched his cheek.

"You're going to be all right," she whispered.

Brian tried to say something, but it came out like the dry rattle of an old man. She leaned closer to listen.

Using all his remaining strength, Brian pushed himself up another inch.

And kissed her.

He held it as long as he could before he fell back to the bed again, passing out.

Chloe froze, refusing to believe what just happened.

He had *kissed* her.

It was a death sentence for a human. Man and Mai had not been able to love each other since the war between them first began, thousands of years ago.

Chloe knew it all too well: she had accidentally killed or almost killed—she still didn't know—a guy she hooked up with at a club before she knew any of this. The last time she had seen Xavier, he was covered in sores and his face was swollen beyond recognition. She had called 911 and fled.

And now, because Brian was convinced he was going to die anyway, he didn't think it would matter.

Six

Chloe managed to sneak back in to her house just as the clock turned five thirty. *Great, a whole two hours of sleep.* She stripped down and fell into a deep slumber almost before she hit the pillow.

She was barely awake two hours later when she came stumbling downstairs. There was her mom, with dough-nuts and coffee for breakfast. She dumped them onto the table, attaché case still slung over her shoulder, and beamed at Chloe.

"They had that chocolate kreme-with-a-*k* you like so much this morning . . . ," Anna started. "Wait, you look *terrible*. What happened?"

"Thanks," Chloe grumbled. That was the humorous part; now came the difficult one. Would she start the whole avalanche of lies all over again? *I'm just really stressed out about my makeup trig exam tomorrow. I could barely sleep.* Two sentences, fourteen—no, fifteen words, and her mom would let the whole thing drop. And if she told the truth? *Hey, Mom, my human boy, uh, friend, well, I found him half dead on the street last night when I was prowling around at 2 a.m., so I took him to the people who sort of held me captive for several weeks.*

She and her mom looked each other in the eye, and each paused too long.

"Well, some coffee will make you feel better," her mom finally said, turning her head quickly away.

Chloe came the rest of the way down the stairs, feeling both infinitely relieved and extremely disturbed. Uncomfortable. *You're not supposed to feel uncomfortable with your mom.* That was for best friends you betrayed with gossip, guys who said they didn't like you back that way, and guidance counselors who were pretty sure you had weed in your locker. You could be *mad* at her . . . but *uncomfortable?* It just didn't seem right.

"Thanks," Chloe said, stuffing her mouth with as much of the doughnut as she could cram in, like she did when she was little. "Hey, shpeaking of . . ." It was hard to form the words around the delicious, thick, totally fake nondairy kreme. "Could you help me study tonight? I want to run some practice proofs."

Chloe meant it as a sort of peace offering to her mom, and it turned out to be exactly the thing to say: Mrs. King smiled, almost as broadly as she had before and tucked a stray wisp of her hair behind her ear. "Absolutely! We'll get Chinese and make a girls' night out of it."

"Girls' night with trig," Chloe said flatly, raising an eyebrow. *Uh-oh, I'm beginning to sound like Kim.*

Her mom leaned over and kissed her on top of her head.

"Girls' night with trig. Gotta run, don't forget to—"

"Lock up, yeah, yeah. Got it."

Chloe watched as her mom grabbed her purse and her glasses and whirlwinded out the door, a dust devil of Ferragamos and Anne Klein. Then she looked down at the rest of her doughnut and sighed.

At school Chloe walked in a daze through the halls, watching the early-morning bustle of students making what use they could of the few free minutes before the day began. The National Honor Society kids were putting up posters about some volunteer thing or other they wanted to get people involved in. The geeks were in a huddle, avidly discussing last night's episode of *Stargate*. The cheerleaders were trying to sell Halloween candygrams to everyone who passed. For a dollar you could send a piece of candy with a note to anyone in the school and have it delivered to his or her homeroom on Halloween morning. In middle school, they had been cheap hard suckers. Now they were little wrapped Godivas.

Every year on Valentine's Day, Easter, Halloween, and Christmas/Hanukkah/Kwanzaa/Diwali, Amy and Chloe had sent each other mysterious notes from "secret admirers," with the sitcom philosophy that boys would see how many candygrams they each got and assume that Amy and Chloe were popular and desirable. Never worked, of course. Not that Amy had even needed them the last few years. *I wonder if she's going to be sending one to Paul?*

"Candygram?" a television-perfect little cheerleader suggested in a peppy voice. Her body was tiny and she wore the home-game uniform, complete with tiny red-and-white skirt. She stood on her toes a little, bouncing.

But Chloe couldn't even work up the energy to hate her; she just shook her head and pushed on. In the open area in the middle of the *X* where the math-science and English-history wings crossed, students were standing on chairs, hanging up autumn-leaf-colored bunting around a giant—and surprisingly tasteful—poster that read *Something Wicked This Way Comes—Get your tickets to the fall formal at lunch! $60/couple, $35/single.*

"What do you think?" Alyec asked, swooping in behind her and kissing Chloe on the cheek.

"I think they're sticking it to people who can't get a date again," Chloe said, hooking her thumbs in her backpack straps.

"Yeah, well, who can't get a date?"

"People who aren't foreign, sexy, and drop-dead gorgeous," she said, kissing him back on the cheek. It was strange: normally they would kiss on the lips if there weren't any of the more monastic teachers or hall

58

monitors about. But right now it just didn't seem right.

Especially after what happened last night. As soon as she had gotten to school, Chloe had called to find out about Brian, but the doctor said he was in the same state, possibly doing a little better than before. No other, "new" symptoms, even when Chloe questioned her carefully. She had to resist calling back every five minutes for an update to make sure the kiss they'd shared wasn't killing him.

"Well, we can't all be lucky." He put his arm around Chloe's shoulders and turned so they could both admire the poster. "I put Hannah Ellington in charge of signage and programs."

"*You* put? I thought you were just on the music committee."

"They all needed some . . . help." It appeared that Alyec was using his powers for good, though: already the event looked like it was going to be better than last year's, less like a stupid high-school dance and more like a college, well, *formal.*

"Did you hear what happened last night?" Chloe asked as they turned and began walking to history. Alyec shook his head. She told him, omitting the part about Brian kissing her. ". . . and if *that* isn't bad enough, I'm having a real hard time wrapping my head around this whole 'being the One' thing. You're supposed to bow to me, you know," she added, elbowing him in the stomach.

"I think the Chosen One's chosen one gets a break," he said, shrugging.

"But you'll still worship me, right?"

"Haven't I always?" He ran his hand back through her hair—like she had done to Brian the night before—and smiled fondly at her. It was a rare moment for him: there was no lust or teasing—just *fondness.*

They walked together to American civ, passing one of the few windows in the hall, which looked out on the strip of dying grass and fence that separated the school from the rest of the world.

Something wasn't quite right. Chloe turned back to look again, but all she saw was what might have been the remains of a footprint in the grass, quickly disappearing as the tough, yellowed stalks sprang back up.

"Hey—did you just see something?" she asked, pulling at Alyec's sleeve and pointing outside.

He frowned. "No—why?"

"I don't know, I just . . ." She shrugged. "I've been getting super creeped out recently. I keep thinking I see someone or someone's following me."

"Nerves. You know what'll fix that?"

"Sex. Yes, I know," Chloe said, laughing.

They sat down at desks next to each other. When they had started dating, he had moved to sit closer to her—a rare thing so late in the term. Chloe was just thinking she might get through the day *normally,* without having to deal with anything really Mai related, when her phone rang. She didn't recognize the number.

"Hello?" she answered it.

"Chloe? It's Sergei."

Chloe's heart sank, her stomach quickly following. Here was another very loose thread from the night of the fight. Yes, Sergei had taken her in and treated her like a daughter, acting like the father she never had, but he might *also* have sent assassins to kill her mom and cut off Chloe from all human contact. And while she was beginning to find that people were a little more complicated than she ever realized before, she still had no desire or ability to deal with the mess that was her relationship with Sergei. Chloe had gotten along recently by forcing herself not to think about the Pride Leader.

"Sergei," she said, feeling her belly twist into ulcerous knots. Alyec raised his eyebrows, listening in.

"You sound well, Chloe."

"I am, thanks. More or less."

"I see you brought us a little visitor last night. . . ." *Here it comes.* Ms. Barker was erasing the board in preparation for class and shooting nasty looks at everyone who was talking on cell phones. Leader of an ancient race of lion people aside, Chloe didn't want to be one of those obnoxious jerks who put a hand up for the teacher to "wait a minute" while finishing a call. She was in enough academic trouble as it was.

". . . I think you and I, and maybe Olga, should get together and have a little chat about things."

"Yeah, uh, sure." She tried to sound upbeat and lighthearted, like that was a great idea.

"When you come to visit your friend today, then?" It wasn't really a question.

"All right."

"Good, I look forward to seeing you later. Good luck in school."

Click.

Chloe slowly closed the phone.

Let's make a deal, she sent a mental message to the Fates or the Twin Goddesses or her biological mom or whoever was casting the dice for her life. *Can you at least switch off crisis weeks? Like, one for school, the next for Amy and Paul, and the next for everything else? Does it all have to happen at once?*

Something hit Chloe's head with a small but pointed *thunk* and snapped her out of her thoughts. Lying on the ground next to her desk was a slightly squished Godiva chocolate. Alyec was grinning wickedly; he must have stolen or sweet-talked it away from the cheerleaders.

Chloe smiled back and whispered a thanks, unwrapping it immediately and popping it in her mouth.

God really does work in mysterious ways, she reflected.

Lunch was a chilly affair that almost made her wish school would hurry up and end so she could face her next set of crap. Chloe sat across from Paul and Amy, who were obviously trying to interact normally—without even touching each other or making eye contact—until the bell rang and Paul gave Amy a perfunctory kiss goodbye. There wasn't so much *tension* at the table as there was a complete freeze on normal, casual behavior. *I knew this would happen,* Chloe thought. When Amy first told her she and Paul had hooked up, it was obvious that, unless they kept dating until college, it could only end in tears for the trio of friends.

She stayed after for an hour to work on one of the many chem labs she'd missed, called "Forming Ionic Compounds." Mrs. Mentavicci was *much* more laid back in these sessions, and when she wasn't grading something—or playing solitaire—she actually helped. Chloe began to see the lure of being tutored. Without the tenseness of a forty-five-minute time limit and having to deal with a lab partner, she was able to work slowly and methodically and actually *understand* what she was doing.

Afterward she took a bus over to Sausalito. Chloe didn't want a car to come pick her up—while luxurious, it was also incredibly disempowering; she felt completely in the Mai's control. It was a good place to think, under the shaky fluorescent bus lights that made everything clearer and more real. Every rivet in the floor, every grommet on the ugly matted upholstery of the seats stood out.

But she could only focus on one thing: There was a chance that Brian could be dead or dying by the time she got to Firebird.

It hadn't been immediate with Xavier, the guy she'd

kissed at the club. When Chloe found him lying on the floor in his apartment a few days later, he was covered in sores and unable to breathe properly—but still alive. Barely. A few more hours—maybe minutes—and he wouldn't have been. She had never followed up on what happened to him. Now was definitely the time to open up that line of inquiry again.

When the bus stopped, Chloe was the only one to get off. The sky was overcast, the clouds high in the atmosphere. Chloe drew as far into her hoodie as she could as a cold wind cut through tree branches and telephone poles. She let her feet slap the ground, willing herself to make ugly, human noises, to challenge the sky and the wind and the graceful lion woman within her. She kicked rocks and pebbles and wished she was thirteen again. Or at least fifteen, before everything had changed.

She reached the gate and realized how tiny she must look against it: a wastrel teenager in a faded sweatshirt and jeans, under a guardhouse that protected one of the largest real estate firms in San Francisco—as well as a dying race of ancient feline warriors.

"Oh, Miss King—would you like me to send a car down to you?"

"No thanks, I'll walk," she said, slipping through the tiny invisible pedestrian "door" that cracked open out of the imposing double gates and led up the long gravel driveway. Chloe couldn't help notice the trees and the topiaries and the bushes and all sorts of beautiful garden things she had never explored while she lived there. She had stayed inside, except for when she escaped to see her friends.

Chloe chose to go around the back, avoiding the lobby and the receptionist and the crowd of people who would be there. Staring at her. Bowing to her. Directing her to Sergei.

Though she didn't remember exactly where the hospital room was, she pieced it together through memory and smell. Chloe tentatively knocked on the door before opening it and going in, as quietly as she had through the gate.

"Hey." Dr. Lovsky was there, checking off something on Brian's chart. She gave a little bow.

Brian was in a slightly different position from when she saw him last and had all sorts of tubes and wires on him. A drip in his arm. Something in his nose. He looked fragile and was the pale color of chicken fat. *Small.*

"How's he doing?" Chloe whispered.

"Talk as loud as you want. He's on so many painkillers, it would take an earthquake to wake him," Dr. Lovsky said, hanging the chart back on the end of his bed. "Stabilized—I'm going to take a closer look at his head today. He's pretty resilient for a human."

"Speaking of human . . ." Chloe closed her eyes and ground her teeth. *A leader isn't afraid to tell the truth.* Think of Washington and the cherry tree. Or Honest Abe. ". . . I probably should have told you this before, but when he thought he was going to die, he, um . . . he kissed me."

Lovsky's clipboard slipped perilously until it was hanging from just one of her claws.

"H-how hard?" she managed to stutter.

"Uh, pretty hard, I guess." Chloe fidgeted. "A teensy bit of tongue," she added, flushing furiously.

"Why didn't you tell me this before?" the doctor shrieked, running a clawed hand over her head. "Honored One."

"Because I thought you would just give up on him—assume he was going to die."

Strangely, Dr. Lovsky didn't argue with that. She seemed to be one of those rare people who didn't protest when they knew the other person was right. "I kissed another boy before I knew who I was, too. . . ."

The other woman just tapped a tooth with her claw.

Chloe cleared her throat. "Is he going to be okay? Can you do something for him?"

The doctor shook her head. "I was . . . involved in a case years ago with a Mai and a human who had only kissed. He died. The hospital couldn't do anything—and it was a damn sight better than anything *here*."

Chloe was cowed into silence—there was definitely a story behind and beyond what she had said.

Calie then frowned, looking puzzled. "But . . . I have seen no evidence of toxic shock or anything even *like* that. *Yet*. It's kind of odd. . . . I'll keep an eye out and

66

prepare some ephedrine." The doctor stomped out, shaking her head and muttering under her breath.

And now, to my doom.

As Chloe made her way upstairs, she played a mental game with herself, trying to decide what she would rather do than meet with Sergei. Pull a hangnail, definitely. Deal with a yeast infection, possibly. Clean her room, almost certainly. Work a midnight sale at Pateena's, absolutely. Spend the afternoon at Aunt Isabel's? Maybe. That was a close one.

Working at Pateena's, much less working midnight sales, weren't really an option anymore, though. Since the owner of the vintage clothing store had told Chloe to not bother coming back at all if she didn't show up on that Wednesday weeks ago, Chloe had given up her job as a complete loss.

She tried to slip past the cheaply dressed receptionist who sat alone at her island of mahogany and dark wood in the middle of the lobby. The only thing keeping her company was a giant vase of expensive flowers.

"He's waiting for you in his office," she said without looking up. *"Honored One."*

Was there the slightest bit of sarcasm in her voice?

Chloe sighed and slunk over to Sergei's door and knocked. The door seemed to open of its own accord, and Olga let her in. Her dark eyes lit up a little when she saw Chloe—but she also looked worried.

"Chloe! Honored One! Come in!" She gave Chloe a

squeeze on the shoulder, not quite a hug. Sergei's right hand was a direct, uncomplicated, and genuine woman; Chloe was pretty sure she knew where she stood with her at all times.

Sergei stood up from behind his desk and gave Chloe a very proper, angular bow. It should have been amusing, considering how short and square he was, but with his heels together and his perfectly trimmed beard he gave the impression of a foreign dignitary. The door clicked shut behind her. *Well, here we go,* Chloe thought, sinking into a chair next to Olga. *If I really am the One, why don't I feel like it?*

"Chloe," Sergei said, sitting back in his chair, "let me begin by saying how glad we are to see you again. We missed you while you were away."

"While I was *home,*" Chloe found herself correcting him. She wished she hadn't. The Fine Art of Making Friends and Influencing People, *not by Chloe King.*

"Yes, while you were home," Sergei said easily, as if it wasn't a concern. "So I take it you're not back for the long haul, as it were?"

There it was. *Wheeeeeeeeee* plop! Like a lit firecracker half dud that lay unexploded between your feet. *Do you pick it up or run?*

"I don't know what my eventual plans are," Chloe said carefully. *Jesus Christ, I'm a sixteen-year-old kid! I shouldn't be having to make decisions about the rest of my life or speak so carefully—politically—to someone three times my age and ten times better at it! I should be dating, fighting with my mom, popping zits in front of the mirror.* "For now, I'm going to live with my mom."

"You gave us a bit of a surprise at the Presidio, leaving with your friends like that," the older man said, eyes flicking briefly to the ground and back up to her as if it were a painful memory. "It really . . . *hurt* me," he added softly.

Chloe felt like vomiting. Right there and then. Was he the greatest actor in the world and *completely* evil—which she sort of preferred at this point—or just a man who had thought he'd found a daughter figure and whose heart had been broken?

"I—I'm sorry. I just . . ."

"It was difficult for you, we understand," Olga said, reaching out to pat her hand. "All the violence must have been a shock."

"But we were there for you, Chloe. You know that, right?" Sergei sort-of pleaded.

There. A little tiny spark of anger. *Grab it, Chlo; follow it down to the source.* It was the only "power" she felt she had right then.

"I *just died,* for Christ's sake! *Again!*" she exploded. "*Tell* me you wouldn't want your mom after something like that."

"Still," Sergei said, crossing his legs and trying a different tactic, "fleeing for a while is completely understandable, as Olga has said. We will always be here, waiting for you. *But bringing a human into our complex?*"

He didn't raise his voice, but it was *cold,* each word ending in sharp silence.

She had been waiting for this, and she was still completely unprepared to answer it.

Chloe opened her mouth, but just then there was a soft click as the door opened behind her. Kim padded silently into the room, as calm and tranquil as a breeze on a sun-soaked oasis. She bowed to Chloe and Sergei and pulled up a chair.

"Kim, this is a private meeting," Sergei said, both baffled and stern.

The girl with the giant black cat ears nodded, smoothing some unseen wrinkle on the front of her long, priest-like black dress. "You are discussing the transition of leadership to the One, correct?" she asked coolly.

"Correct," Sergei answered through gritted teeth.

"I too must cede my power—I no longer represent the spiritual body of this Pride. Chloe is now the high priestess. This must be discussed as well." She sat down, and that was the end of the story.

THANK YOU! Chloe thought at Kim. *A thousand times, thank you.* If the other girl noticed Chloe looking at her, she ignored it, as if it was all just business as usual. But there was the slightest gleam in her eye that the two adults didn't notice.

Now, if being the One came with cat ears and a tail or something else visually freaky, I'd be able to pull stunts like that without batting an eyelash, too, Chloe thought a little jealously. Kim got away with a *lot* because of her ingrained weirdness.

The leader of the Pride let out a large sigh, as if he was giving up, changing his previous stance. "Chloe, this is just really hard. For a number of reasons," he said frankly, "besides the personal ones—I *really do* want you back here. I *like* our little chess games and chats and . . . having you around," he added quickly, as if he was a little embarrassed. Whatever else was true about him, the lion-haired middle-aged man really did like her, but did he like her so much that he had tried to kill her mom to keep her?

"And think of me," he went on, gesturing to the walls around him. "I spent my *entire life* and millions of dollars building this little safe haven for us, this little real estate empire, and bringing our people over. It's a little strange to suddenly have to hand it all over to a young girl."

"I don't think Chloe needs to involve herself with the business part of our Pride," Kim suggested in a tone that made it sound more like a statement of the obvious. "At least not yet. It's not really part of her 'job description' anyway. She is our *spiritual* leader, leader in all things having to do with the Mai. Not humans."

"What does that mean?" Olga asked bluntly.

"Well, in ancient days, she would have led us in the rites and rituals of the Twin Goddesses," Kim said thoughtfully. "Or led us to war against out enemies. Or led the Hunt. Sacrificed herself, if need be, for the

71

continued survival of the Pride. Now it means leading the Pride in whatever direction it needs to survive—and thrive—*today* in the modern era, in this new world."

Olga, Sergei, and Kim looked expectantly at Chloe, who still had no idea what that meant. What *would* she suggest they do to become "more modern"? *Get an MP3-player hooked up to the speaker system in the lounge, maybe?*

"The first thing I think we should do is hold an all-Pride gathering," Sergei decided. "A meeting where we introduce you to everyone properly. There are those who won't believe you're the One until they've seen you in person. Kim, you should give her a crash course in our spirituality and the rites of the Twin Goddesses. I'll fill you in on how we've been more or less governing ourselves for the past few decades." He gave Chloe a weak smile. "As well as the traditions of leadership and the kizekh. We could order pizza . . . ?"

A peace offering. He really did want her back—if only part time.

"Okay," Chloe said, nodding, trying to look like it was no big deal.

"Good—can we meet this Friday?" Chloe shrugged. Sounded fine. "And we should have the gathering soon thereafter." He flipped a page on his desk calendar. "Tuesday, maybe."

"Shouldn't you check everyone's schedules first?"

Chloe found herself saying. Even Kim had difficulty not rolling her eyes.

"Chloe King," Sergei said mock-sternly, "the first thing you should know about the Pride is that this is *not* a democracy."

Not a democracy. As Chloe followed Kim back to the sanctuary where the cat gods Bastet and Sekhmet were worshiped, those words repeated themselves over and over in her mind.

Okay, let's play this game. Pretend I'm leader of this entire group of felines. What do I think is best for them? Chloe asked herself.

Integrate more, was the immediate and loudest answer. There must be a way to survive racially and socially and not resort to holing up in a mansion on the outskirts of town like vampires. Play video games. Go to the movies. Make everyone go to college.

"Kim, I have no idea what these people expect me to do as the One or even what I *should* do," she admitted aloud, sitting down on a bench as Kim bowed and said a little prayer to each of the goddesses: Bastet, house cat with the gentle smile and the earring; Sekhmet, with her teeth bared. The only sound in the room was the "moat" that separated the goddesses' dais from the rest of the room, a gentle trickle of water meant to remind worshipers of the Nile.

"What you should do will come with time," Kim said,

73

shrugging. "You are only sixteen and the world is much more complicated than it was in the days of hunting and gathering. As for the expectations of others, the wise will understand. Everyone else will have to be patient."

"What am I supposed to do in the meantime? If you asked me what I would do *today,* I would say breathe some fucking *air* and light into this place. Uh . . . not the temple, I mean Firebird," she added quickly as Kim frowned. " 'Sergei was right: the Mai *shouldn't* be trapped here. They should be free to interact with the rest of the world and control their own destinies instead of being bound to some five-thousand-year-old curse. *And* a boring real estate company."

Kim watched her curiously, listening without judgment.

"If it were up to me," Chloe said slowly, thinking of Xavier and Brian, "I would do everything possible to get rid of the curse. That would be my number-one goal. It's not fair to us *or* the humans we might accidentally wind up with. And besides that, it really adds to the whole cultish aspect of the Pride. No mixing with humans means a lot of dating at home and—well, pressure to keep it in the family. Having the place where you live for only a few years destroyed so you're forced to move on makes everyone clingy, to a leader as well as each other. Lions roam free over hundreds of miles, going where and with whom they please . . . staying in their pride because they want to, not because they're forced, you know?"

Actually, Chloe didn't know if that last part was true, but it sounded good. In the dreams she had there was a sense of power and freedom that was definitely missing from her own close Pride. Kim nodded, looking almost hungry for that freedom.

"But let's say we do that, huh?" Chloe said, slumping. "We somehow get rid of the curse, Mai and humans can interact again, everyone goes off and lives happily ever after on their own. The freedom of the Mai means their eventual integration and disappearance. I mean, there are six billion humans to meet and fall in love with and have babies with. The Mai would cease to exist in a couple of generations—is *that* the right thing? How can you have complete individual freedom and still maintain the culture of the Mai?"

A small smile curled at the edge of her friend's lips, and her ears dipped a little. "Chloe, I think maybe you have answered your original question. Perhaps a *spiritual* guide who keeps us all connected is what is called for in this age."

Chloe blinked.

"Anyway, you still have that five-thousand–year-old curse to lift, people to win over, and French to pass, so your plate's pretty full right now, as they say," Kim added, lighting a candle and picking up a handful of sand to continue her benedictions.

"Yeah, thanks for helping me," Chloe said a little glumly, brought back from her philosophical daydreams about the future to the reality of schoolwork. "And thanks for crashing the meeting, too, by the way. Things with Sergei were getting a little tense."

"No problem." It was strange hearing modern phrases come out of Kim's mouth with her little fangs showing.

"But of course he's going to be a little weird about just handing over leadership of this Pride to a sixteen-year-old, right?" Chloe looked to her friend expectantly. "I mean, who wouldn't be?"

Kim paused in her ritual and stared at Chloe unblinkingly, for a long enough time that Chloe actually began to feel uncomfortable.

"Hey, drink up," Alyec said, toasting her and tipping back a frosty mug of India Pale Ale.

Chloe looked around the library, realizing how much she'd missed the Thursday night cocktail parties at Firebird. Everyone was dressed up and taking drinks that were served on silver trays. The older Mai who had grown up in Abkhazia or Russia or Georgia had straight champagne and expensive shots of vodka in glasses made of ice.

Igor, Valerie, Alyec, and the other younger members of the Pride tended to drink beer, but Chloe was enamored of the sophisticated drinks she could never afford, the ones that they talked about in magazines and *Sex and the City:* pink cosmopolitans, three-olive dirty martinis, Bellinis with champagne and peach nectar.

When she'd lived there, Sergei had always watched

Chloe carefully and never let her have more than one. So she sipped slowly.

I'm the One now, though. Doesn't that mean I'm old enough to drink?

It was pretty amazing, she thought as she sat on a velvet love seat among the younger members. Here she was in a library out of a mystery novel that was full of lion people—her *own* people—a secret feline race living among humans and all of them gorgeous.

"I want a full veil," Valerie announced, throwing a much-thumbed *Martha Stewart Weddings* magazine down onto the coffee table for all to see.

So much for the cool, sexy, secret stuff. Chloe sighed, but she looked at the page interestedly.

"That's a patriarchal tradition for this day and age," said Simone. She was the beautiful, red-haired dancer Chloe met at the hunt. When she moved—even casually—it was hard for anyone, male or female, to take eyes off her. "Though the lace is pretty."

"Patriarchal, whatever, bah. This is what I want."

"Whatever you want, it shall be yours," Igor said, kissing her on the forehead.

Alyec and Chloe smiled at each other, rolling their eyes.

"Kim suggested adding some traditional Mai stuff," Simone pressed. "You going to do that?"

The couple looked at each other, lips pursed in thinking expressions. "I think it's a good idea," Igor finally said. Valerie nodded.

Chloe had just sat through one group "service" that Kim led—it was always a personal religion, the cat-eared girl had emphasized, but a surprising number of Mai showed up. Instead of psalmbooks there were scrolls in languages Chloe couldn't read. Some of the service was in English, but most was in Russian and Mai. Kim had poured out little measures of dried meat—it looked suspiciously like cat food—and honey and wine at the base of each statue. Kind of interesting, from an anthropological perspective, but not something Chloe really felt she could get worked up about.

"But you have to throw a bouquet," one of the other girls said. "That way one of us unmarried girls can catch it."

"Agreed." Valerie laughed.

"Are you going to have your father bring you down the aisle?" Chloe asked, thinking about other possible "patriarchal" aspects of the service.

"I don't know who my father is," Valerie said, shrugging. "He's probably dead."

"Oh," Chloe said. "I don't know mine either."

The other girl nodded, as if it were obvious.

"It's funny . . . ," Chloe said slowly, thinking about it. "Everyone is all concerned about finding out who my biological *mom* is, but no one has said anything about my dad."

"Uh, Honored One." Simone coughed delicately.

"Lineage in the Mai is always determined through the *mother* because you always know who your mother is."

"Yeah, but—"

Alyec cut in. "What she is trying to say, Chloe, is that in the past your husband was not always the father of all your children."

She knew it was impolite, but Chloe couldn't help gaping. Was this a cat-legacy thing? Or was it just a result of the violence and chaos in Eastern Europe?

Somehow Chloe didn't think it was the latter. The implications were . . . not nice images.

"So, have you and Alyec talked at all?" Valerie asked, changing the subject. "You know, about this?"

Alyec began to choke on his beer.

"I'm sixteen!" Chloe said, stunned at the implications of the woman's question.

"Oh, I didn't mean *now*," she said, laughing heartily. "But do you, you know . . . have any plans? Going steady?"

Everyone was staring at her and Alyec interestedly, even Igor. Her boyfriend was completely silent for once and seriously blushing.

Suddenly Chloe got it. There were fewer Mai than Rhode Islanders—probably fewer than the Amish. Every couple was a pair of potential breeders.

"Oh, look at the time! Gotta go," she said without attempting to disguise the lame excuse.

"Yeah, I've got to go find my mom. Uh, early night," Alyec said instantly, also getting up.

"Oh, Chloe, you are so funny," Valerie said. "You too, Alyec. You're a *perfect* couple."

The perfect couple left as quickly as possible without knocking furniture over or books off their shelves.

"Well, uh, good night," Alyec said when they were outside.

"Uh, yeah." Chloe kissed him, but it was short and sort of perfunctory. He didn't hold it either. When they finally looked into each other's eyes, they laughed nervously.

Seven

A = 33 degrees, B = 95 degrees, a = 6 cm
What is the length of b?

In the last couple of months, Chloe had grown claws, fought an assassin, died twice, and become the leader of her people. It just didn't seem fair that she had to deal with *this* as well.

She took a deep breath, thinking about the late-night study session she'd had with her mom. *Law of sines.*

$$a/\sin A = b/\sin B$$
$$6/\sin 33 = b/\sin 95$$
$$6/0.5446 = b/0.9962$$
$$b = {\sim}10.97$$

That seemed right.

Chloe heaved a deep sigh and peeled the exam off her desktop, where it had stuck from the pressure and hand sweat. Maybe elbow sweat, too.

She handed it to Mr. Hyde, the calculus and computer teacher who had been quietly waiting for her at his desk, solving a puzzle in *Scientific American.* He took the test from her as if he had forgotten she was there, faintly surprised and pleased. He was ascetically thin and all Vulcan, except for the ears and the sense of humor. All arching eyebrows and flawless logic.

"Listen," he said, a little louder than his usual soft-spoken self. "I was kind of thinking of having you as an alternate on the math team next marking period, after Christmas."

Chloe almost dropped her books again. *Her?* She wasn't a geek—just kind of good at math. Or at least better than a lot of other sophomores.

"I don't know. . . . I've never been much of a joiner."

"Just think about it, okay?" he begged. "I'd really like you on the team. You'd be a great role model to younger girls."

"Uh, sure. See ya." Chloe got out of the classroom as quickly as she could, waving her hand behind her. *Her* on the math team? *If one more thing gets freaky in my life, just* one more thing, *I swear I'm gonna—*

"Hey, Chloe. You look like you've seen a ghost," Paul called out to her. He was flipping through the comic books that he had just bought, brown bag under his arm.

"Jekyll and Hyde just basically asked me to join the math team. As an alternate," she added quickly.

"I didn't know trig was one of your superpowers. Speaking of, how are things over at the cathouse?"

"They want me to be their leader." Chloe leaned against the wall and slid down it until she was sitting on the floor. Paul followed suit. She dug through her bag, hoping for a candy bar or something, but only found an old cough drop. It was a little dusty from being at the bottom of her bag, but she unwrapped it and popped it into her mouth anyway. Cherry. Her favorite. "You?"

"My dad has a girlfriend," he said, staring at the floor with large, unblinking eyes.

Okay. That was officially "it." The last freaky thing.

"How long?" she asked, also staring at the floor. Paul got embarrassed easily and he looked dangerously close to freaking out, so it seemed the safest thing to do.

"I . . . I don't know. I think they knew each other—I know they knew each other—she's the daughter of some friends of my parents."

Daughter!

"Korean?"

"Yeah. A lot more . . . traditional than my mom. *And* a lot younger," he added with an angry smile. "She's my dad's new secretary."

"Oh, you are *shitting* me," Chloe sympathized.

Some of the anger drained out of his smile and it became broader, if sadder. "I don't think they actually had an affair before my parents began the divorce—I don't even know if they're sleeping together now. She still lives at home with her parents—she's thirty-*two.*"

They sat quietly for a moment, side by side. That seemed like all Paul really wanted: someone to listen and understand and not react. Chloe understood the feeling all too well.

"Would—would you do me a favor?" he asked, sniffing a little.

She nodded.

"Don't tell Amy?"

Chloe felt her stomach freeze. This was the beginning of a whole new "it."

"I'll tell her myself, but not yet—I just found out, and . . ."

Of course it made sense: things were already weird between her two best friends. Now was not the time for further complications, sympathy, or anger. But he had made Chloe his confidante—once again the three of them were split two to one, but this time Amy was the odd man out.

And if she ever finds out I knew about this before her and didn't tell, I'm toast.

"Yeah, whatever. Sure," Chloe said.

They sat there for a few minutes, not speaking. Chloe looked down the empty hall of the math wing, so silent, it was almost like it had already been evacuated for the summer or Christmas vacation. Long rows of green and blue lockers, recently repainted, reflected glossily in the tiles of the floor, extending their length six feet into a blurrier universe. Doors were left open here and there and the very slightest hint of fresh air managed to tunnel through the ancient smells of paste, dirt, textbooks, and copy paper.

Very soon, Chloe realized, this would all be a memory. Whatever happened with the rest of her life, as a cat or as a human, less than three quick years would pass and all that would remain of these turbulent days were memories, like this silent, still image of her and Paul on the floor.

A bell rang and there was a school-wide shuffling and shifting as those who stayed late or were in detention finally got to go free. Chloe rose to her feet and pulled Paul with her with the ease of her Mai strength.

"I dare you to give me a piggyback ride," he said weakly.

"Don't tempt me." Chloe smiled. "You know, I could have your dad's girlfriend killed," she said brightly as they began to walk down the hall together. "I know an entire organization of assassins now. Two organizations, actually."

"As much as I don't want to sound like a sensitive New Age boy," Paul said with a sigh, "I *think* my dad might have something to do with this as well. You know?"

When they got to the lobby, Amy saw them and waved; she had something that looked suspiciously like a giant portfolio under her arm.

"Hey, guys. How are things?" It sounded forced. Even for Amy.

"Not too shabby," Chloe answered, shrugging.

"How's Brian?"

Chloe tapped her tooth, remembering at the last moment to keep her claws sheathed. It was really much more satisfying the other way, but they were in public. Finally she decided. If she had no control over the rest of her life, at least she could keep things clear with her friends.

"He kissed me."

Both of her friends' jaws dropped, and Chloe wished they could see themselves. They actually made a pretty good couple. It sucked that they were breaking up, considering Chloe was just getting used to them as an item.

"He's not dead," she said shakily, hoping it was still true. It had been at least two hours since she last called Dr. Lovsky. "And he hasn't shown any symptoms yet, either. They've got him pretty closely monitored, so if he goes into anaphylactic shock, at least they'll be able to catch it. He was a *dumbass*," she added before Amy could open her mouth. "I guess he thought he was going to die—he was so out of it from the blood loss."

"Holy cow," Paul said, shocked beyond the realm of swear words. "*Sooo* glad I didn't wind up with you for two minutes in the closet at Amy's thirteenth birthday party."

"Life sucks," Chloe said, letting the misery descend on her for one brief moment, in the safety of her friends. Then she shook her head. "I've got to find out what happened to Xavier."

Amy shrugged. "I've been checking the newspapers and public police records online every day since you asked a couple of weeks ago—nothing has come up about him yet. There was one obituary for a Xavier Constantine, but he was eighty-seven."

"Well, that's good news, I guess. Not for the old guy, I mean."

"Are you going to check out his apartment? See if he's even still there?" Paul asked.

She shook her head. "Not tonight. I'm . . . kind of exhausted. I'm just going to go home." Chloe wasn't sure she would be able to deal with it if she found out Xavier was dead—one of the reasons she had been putting it off for so long.

"Oh, you're busy tonight," Amy said, a little too quickly. She turned to Paul. "You want to hang, maybe? Watch the *Star Trek* marathon?"

As clichéd as it was, Chloe realized this was a train wreck she could only watch. She kept hoping her friends would not say the inevitable. *Superhuman strength, night vision, and no way to salvage the next minute of conversation.* She sighed.

Paul shifted uncomfortably. "Not tonight."

That's one. . . .

"Other plans?" Amy pushed, still trying to sound bright.

That's two. . . .

"No, I just . . . I don't think it's a good idea right now."

That's three!

Between Amy's constant pressure and Paul's stupidly excessive honesty at the wrong time, it was amazing they hadn't spontaneously combusted earlier. Chloe found herself actually closing her eyes and wincing.

"Oh," Amy said, color rushing to her cheeks.

"Well, I gotta get going," Paul said, pretending to ignore everything that had just happened. He reshouldered his messenger bag—this one said *Aladdin Sane* on it—and went through the emergency exit that hadn't been hooked to an alarm system since the seventies, when students started toking up in the alley. *Exit the cowardly hero, stage left.*

"I have to go to the dance meeting," Amy said shakily, too shocked and upset to react yet.

"*You?* You're on the fall formal committee?" Chloe asked with more surprise than was strictly necessary, trying to get her friend to smile.

"Alyec bet me I couldn't do a better job than Mrs. Dinan. . . ."

"I'll go with you," Chloe volunteered, thinking about what a smart guy her boyfriend was.

The gym was decorated with little dots of students in socks and bare feet—*No Street Shoes*—with charts and clipboards, pointing at this set of bleachers and that basketball net, joined by the art teacher, who waved her arm around like she was painting the ceiling. A pile of fake ravens was thrown into a corner, bags of little evil glowing plastic spiders and caterpillars next to it. Probably favors or something. It was the only time Chloe had actually seen anyone excited about anything in the gym. But through the windows and skylights she could see that the sky was bleakly heading toward sunset, the layers of white clouds like dryer lint after a load of whites. This was the downside of fall—Halloween, leaves, apples, cider, and the beginning of the party season aside, this was a little bit of the autumn that set in before Thanksgiving and lasted through Christmas: dark and drear, cold and snowless.

Chloe led her friend to the closest set of risers, where she could cry in relative peace.

"We haven't—he hasn't *said* anything definite . . . ," Amy murmured, the tears finally coming.

"Sounds like he pretty much just did," Chloe said as gently as she could. But sometimes her friend got so wrapped up in her own emotions, she wasn't able to clearly see what was actually going on around her.

"Hey, pretty ladies." Alyec neatly vaulted straight up over the side and onto the step where they sat, with an ease and grace that was completely inhuman. No one in the gym was watching. Amy sniffed back a tear; Chloe knew she liked being let in on the Mai's secret lives, that even *Alyec* trusted her with it. But she still quickly lifted her bright green scarf to cover her face and blot her eyes.

"Hey, we're waiting for you."

"I still can't believe you're doing this . . . ," Chloe muttered.

Amy was still blowing her nose and trying to hide her tears; Alyec answered for her. "Yup, she's helping with the overall installation. The gestalt, if you will. Putting the 'Wicked' in 'Something Wicked This Way Comes.'" There was an extraloud sniff behind the scarf. "Hey, what's wrong?" Alyec asked nonchalantly. "And where's your little friend?"

Chloe whacked him with the back of her hand.

"What, he finally came out of the closet?" Alyec asked, faking concern.

"He's not *gay*," Amy protested, blowing her nose and crumpling the napkin up. "It would be easier if he was," she added weakly.

"Well, he does have a bit of the mama's boy," Alyec said. "I mean, he's nice and all, but not exactly a *stud*. Oh, come *on*." He grabbed the tasseled ends of Amy's scarf and tugged them a little. "I'll bet he never really got your juices going, someone like *you*. . . ." He pulled Amy in and suddenly dipped her so low that her frizzy hair was inches away from the wooden benches, his face inches from hers.

"What are you *doing?*" Amy demanded, the sadness momentarily banished from her face.

"Cheering you up. I could kiss your tears away if you wanted, but that would be fatal—wouldn't it?"

The two were frozen there for a long moment.

Neither Alyec nor Amy blinked or looked away. Tension crackled.

Chloe found herself staring, too. And then she found herself getting *really annoyed*.

"Let me up, douche bag," Amy finally snapped, breaking the spell.

"As madam commands; I live to serve." With one fluid curve of his arm he pulled her upright, then brought it below his stomach for a formal bow.

"Thanks for, uh, staying with me," Amy said, turning to Chloe. "And for the little lesson about how *all* men suck," she added with a glare at Alyec, then marched off toward the art teacher, who now looked like she was conducting an invisible orchestra with a large paint-brush she had found somewhere.

Chloe watched her friend go; as angry as her steps were, she still fidgeted nervously with her scarf and the places where Alyec had touched her.

"WHAT THE HELL WAS THAT?" Chloe demanded, turning back to him.

"I was cheering her up, like I said." He sat down on the step above her and picked up a flyer that someone had left there, as though the incident was almost completely forgotten.

"*Alyec.*" Chloe tore the paper out of his hand so hard that her claws threatened to come out.

"I wasn't really going to kiss her," he said innocently. "I don't want her dead."

"You weren't really *joking* about kissing her either, were you?"

The silence between them was as deep and long as the one between him and Amy—but for very different reasons.

"Chloe," he said with a smile, "you knew I was a flirt. You've *always* known I'm a flirt. It came free with purchase."

Chloe glowered. She knew what he said was true, but still . . . It was one thing when it was Keira and Halley and whoever else. He'd *told* her he didn't really feel anything for them—besides the unavoidable fact that they were human. But her best friend? And *right in front of her?*

"And what if you *could?*" she demanded, thinking of Brian and Xavier and her talk with Kim. "Would you have?"

"Chloe, why are you getting so pissed?" he asked, frowning. "Nothing happened—I really was just cheering your friend up."

But she didn't believe it. There was definitely something different between him and Amy than the other girls. For one thing, she hated him. And for another, the opposite of love isn't hate. It's indifference.

"I just—" She couldn't put it into words. She was just pissed. That was all—she didn't like what she had seen and it had pissed her off and he was her *boyfriend,* for chrissake.

"I didn't realize you were so jealous," he said, a little

coolly. "Do you really think you have a right—what about that sick human lover of yours?"

It hit her like a slap; he had never spoken to her that way before. But from the day she first saw her claws, the afternoon when she was on the phone with Brian and IM'ing with Alyec, she knew this moment was coming. It was all fun and games with two boyfriends, two different races, one in love with her and one, well, in "fun" with her, but now was the moment of reckoning.

"Fair enough," she said, swallowing and choking back tears, the same way Amy had just a few minutes earlier with Paul.

"I know the way you feel about him," Alyec continued quietly. She had finally gotten beneath his carefree, joking exterior, and *this* was how. *Happy now, Chlo?* "I keep hoping you'll change your mind. But whatever we have, even if it's just for kicks, it would be nice if you kept the same rules for everyone."

Run away.

It was a powerful instinct; she hurt and didn't know what to do or say. She fought it; she was the One, right? She had faced down psycho-killer assassins before.

"Fine," Chloe said through a clenched jaw. "You're right." She stood up and shouldered her bag. "I have to think about this. I'm going home now."

"Chloe," Alyec said, a little more gently, a lot more uncertainly. "I didn't mean for us to fight about this—"

"No, you're right. I shouldn't keep the two of you

dangling. It's wrong. I'm going home, good night," she said with finality, and walked off to the bus stop.

Chloe had only gone for the bus to put some literal space between her and Alyec, but she got off after a couple of stops. The only time she had to think anymore was when in transit, and she wanted to make it last as long as possible. In the cold dusk air, by herself, the irrational passion drained away. True, the whole Alyec-Brian thing would have to be worked out sometime, eventually, but that wasn't the real issue of the fight.

The real issue was how she *couldn't* have a relationship with Brian. The real issue was a stupid curse because she was Mai and because of things that people had done five millennia ago. Chloe was suddenly overcome with panic and she froze: she really could be responsible for the deaths of Xavier and Brian. They could really die or already be dead.

She shook herself and ran a hand over her face and scratched her scalp, extending her claws, trying to snap herself out of it. *This had all better—*

Chloe stopped, suddenly aware of an almost-noise. Something so slight it could have been missed even by her Mai hearing or dismissed as some random night noise—a mouse, a rat, a can being blown—but it ended too sharply. Like the moment she noticed it. A very slight crunching of gravel, a . . .

She started walking again, picking up the pace. If it was a mugger or rapist or whatever, she had no doubt she could handle herself. But those were monsters of the past; the things she feared now were more complicated and dangerous. She shook her head and kept walking.

What I really need is a vacation. Yeah, that was it. The sort of place inspired by sequined flip-flops, flowery beach bags, expensive sunblock, and fruity drinks. She and her mom could go somewhere fun for Thanksgiving instead of Grandma and crazy Aunt Isabel's; maybe bring a lot of good, crappy books, lie out on the beach, *swim.* . . .

There it was again.

Perfectly matched with her own footsteps.

"Okay, come on out!" she yelled, planting her feet and resting her thumbs around her backpack straps. "You *sure* picked the wrong day to screw with me!"

A low wind hit her coldly in the shins and made ripping noises as it tore through fenders, hydrants, and other metal obstacles. Pebbles eddied around Chloe's feet like they were caught in an invisible wave. A man rode slowly past on a Vespa, staring at the crazy teen in the street. His headlight had no power against the gray in the air and lit up nothing besides itself.

"I *warned* you! We have a truce," she shouted. The wind shifted direction and threw the words back into her own face; her voice couldn't have carried more than a few feet.

No one appeared or owned up to making any noises.

"This sucks," Chloe muttered. "I am *out* of here."

And *then* she turned and ran.

Eight

"Hey, Mom," Chloe said wearily, closing the door behind her. It was only half an act. She threw her book bag onto the counter and went over to the fridge, looking for something easy, filling, and comforting.

"Bag off the counter," her mom said without looking up from the magazine she was reading on the couch—*Utne Reader.* "I have some risotto from Lixia's we can nuke and a salad, so don't spoil your appetite."

Carbs. Nice, warm, comforting carbs. Just what Chloe wanted. She grabbed a Diet Coke with lime and wandered over to the couch, where she plopped down, head in her mom's lap and feet propped up on the armrest.

Anna King looked over the magazine at her daughter. "Hard day at work? How was your exam?"

"Oh, that was *fine*. It's everything else that sucks." Chloe ticked off things on her fingers. "Paul and Amy are breaking up. I think Alyec might like Amy. Paul's dad is already dating his secretary. I have two boyfriends, both of whom are kind of . . . burdens right now. Mr. Hyde—not even my own *teacher*, mind you—wants me to be on the math team. And according to Kim, I'm supposed to lead my lion people into a new age of spiritual enlightenment."

"Paul's dad is dating his *secretary?*" Chloe's mom said excitedly, leaning forward and putting her magazine down.

"Mom . . ."

"I know, honey. It's just . . ." Her mother's eyes unfocused, trying to imagine. "*That* little piece of fluff? She's like an anime character. One of the evil ones."

"While I appreciate the teen-appeal metaphor, can we please get back to me now?"

"Being on the math team will look *great* on your applications." Anna began to play with her daughter's hair, twirling a stray lock with her finger and trying to fix it to the top of her head under another lock.

"So would being the leader of a clandestine race of human feline warriors," Chloe growled.

"I suppose . . . ," her mother said carefully, "if we couched it in different terms, like that girl did in her speech for *Whale Rider*. Actually, that would be a *great* essay—how you looked for your biological roots as a teen and found far more than you ever expected. . . ."

"Mom." Chloe sat up and looked her mother right in the eye. "They really want me to *lead* them. You know, *lead?*"

There was a long pause. Her mother opened her mouth and blinked a few times, stalling—something Chloe had never seen her do before. Attorney Anna King was almost never at a loss for words. Even when she was the victim of kidnapping.

"Better make sure you get into Berkeley, then," she finally said with a faint smile. Then she squared her jaw and her look turned serious. "Chloe, I know I don't understand everything that's going on with you and the other . . . *Mai,* or even have anything to do with it. It's more than obvious what some of your other . . . *friends* and people think of me, your *human* mother. But whatever you decide to do, do it educated. Foreign kings and royalty have always sent their children, princes and princesses and whatever, here for college. You would make a much better leader of your people with a university degree."

Chloe thought about this, sinking back into the couch. "I don't think Sergei would mind keeping a heavier hand in until I'm ready."

"He's the one with the red hair and the gun?"

"Uh, just a gun that one time. Usually it's claws."

"It looked like he was trying to shoot me. Or Brian. Or that other boy," her mother said levelly.

"At least he didn't kidnap you," Chloe countered weakly. "Are you going to try to press charges? Against the Order of the Tenth Blade?"

Her mother made a nasty face. "Who would I have

99

for witnesses? Are your Mai going to stand up for me in court? And Brian—who seems to be the only decent one of the lot—has disappeared."

Chloe winced guiltily. All cat business aside, if she revealed to her mother that "the only decent one of the lot"—and sort of her boyfriend—had been beaten half to death by his own friends . . . Well, it would just confuse the whole dating issue more, and that would definitely make Chloe's life even more complicated.

"I can't believe you're just going to drop it."

"I didn't say I was going to drop it," her mother answered, almost absently. "I just have to . . . figure out the right strategy."

For the first time in the last few months, Chloe suddenly wondered if her mother was hiding something from *her*. Something strange, illegal, or awful. *Parents with secrets* . . . Not a comforting thought. Which reminded her.

"Hey, do you think Dad knew anything about what I am?"

Anna King was knocked out of her reverie. "No, I don't think—" Then she stopped, shifting on the couch uncomfortably. "All of our fights about how to raise you—he even wanted to give you back to your own people at one point. I just thought he meant the Russians," she said slowly. "He was so . . . adamant about certain things. Way, *way* too overprotective—"

"And then he disappeared. So there's a chance,"

Chloe interrupted with more bitterness than she'd intended. Maybe her dad had skipped town to avoid the assassinations, the kidnappings, and the general craziness of being caught between the Tenth Bladers and the Mai. Or maybe he was just trying to protect Chloe—the man who knew too much getting out so she could live a more normal life. *Maybe he thought Mom was safer not knowing about anything.*

Suddenly Chloe was exhausted. She fell back into her mom's lap again. "Did I mention Paul and Amy are breaking up?"

"A little too weirdly timed, with his parents and all, don't you think?"

Her mom reached over for the cup of coffee she had been sipping from. Unlike many things in the house, it was old and the handle had broken off and been glued carefully back on almost ten years ago. It was a dark aqua, kind of out in household furnishings since the early eighties, and clashed with all of the jade- and turquoise-themed pieces that fit into Mrs. King's New Southwest style.

Out of place, old, and infinitely comforting. Her mom had used that mug since before Chloe could remember. She closed her eyes, squidging her butt more comfortably into the couch.

"So they're not going to the fall formal together?" her mother continued, after a loud sip. "Maybe he'll take you. Or all three of you could go together or something. I went to my junior prom with my best friends. We pretended we were Charlie's Angels, under-cover. With potato pellet guns."

"Oh, those wacky seventies." Chloe tried not to think of Alyec. She and Paul and Amy only ever went to dances when Amy dragged them. If Brian lived—*when Brian got better*—she would really have to decide what to do about him. Them. *Us.* Things had gotten too serious. Of course, there was still the question of Mai and humans and toxic kisses; just because Brian hadn't died immediately didn't mean there weren't long-term effects.

Chloe sighed.

It was time to visit Xavier.

She didn't have to scramble around her messy room desperately looking for his address this time; whether it was another Mai ability or something she'd always had and never used, Chloe had no problem remembering exactly where the apartment was—by landmark and general direction, though, not street names and house numbers.

She went immediately after school the next day; no makeup classes that afternoon. It was nice to get away from everything. *I really do need a little more "me" time,* Chloe reflected unironically as she skipped up the steps to the old house. *And not just running at night across the skyline.* She needed a good book or a hobby or to get out on the mountain bike her mom had given her for her sixteenth birthday.

Chloe rang the doorbell, her scarf unfurling behind her in the October breeze. Then, without even asking who she was, Xavier—or someone—clicked the thing that unlocked the door and Chloe went in.

Just three floors until I find out if Xavier is alive or dead.

She rushed up the stairs two at a time, trying to make as much headway as she could before her nerves failed her. Once again the old-house smell of wood and lemony cleaner made her ache to live in a beautiful house like this, even if it was just an apartment. She *hated* her house—it looked like every other piece of two-story urban ranch mediocrity out there. One of the things that first drew her to living with the Mai at Firebird was waking up in an old gabled nook with perilously warped wood plank floors and the dusty quietude only an old house could have.

When she got to the right landing, Xavier's door was already open a crack. She knocked anyway, not wanting to just walk in. Not like last time.

"It's open . . . ," came a voice from inside. The voice was male—but she couldn't tell if it was Xavier's or not. It was hard to hear anything right now over the fast and heavy heartbeats that drummed in her chest—and the only words they'd exchanged had been shouted at the top of their lungs in the club and whispered outside in the parking lot.

The apartment looked almost exactly like it had the night she had come upon him rolling on the floor, dying. A few extra magazines were scattered around, a new candle placed on a windowsill. Still spare, expensive, casual, and Euro-bachelor-y. From the scraping sound of a pan and a spatula, Chloe decided he was probably in the middle of cooking something. . . . But was it him?

"Oh." Xavier came in from the kitchen, dish towel under his chin and pan in one hand, spatula in the other.

Chloe almost threw up with relief. He was alive. And okay.

More than okay, actually. Chloe was shocked by how good-looking he was even in daylight: raven black hair, lovely tan skin, and eyes an incredibly, amazingly light brown. Very exotic. He wore jeans and an impossibly crisp white T-shirt, like he was just preparing for a "casual" model shoot.

"Chloe—right?" he said, raising his perfectly formed eyebrows. "The girl from the club?"

She was floored that he could remember. As far as she knew, he was just a rich foreign college student who was into picking up random American high-school girls. Her heart was finally calming down; for a moment there it was fifty-fifty she was going to pass out.

"Uh, yeah." Chloe had had no actual plan for when she actually met him, if he was still alive. Now that she had seen him, all she wanted to do was rush back and see Brian. There was hope.

"Have you eaten yet?"

Eaten yet? It was two thirty. Lunch? Tea? Elevensies?

"Uh, I'm fine, thanks," she said awkwardly. Her hands itched for her cell phone.

"So." He put the pan carefully down on a coffee table. "I haven't seen you at The Bank, but then again, I haven't been there much recently myself," he said, referring to the club where she met him on the eve of her sixteenth birthday.

"You've been sick," Chloe said as neutrally as she could, making it sound like both a question and a statement.

"How did you know?" He looked up at her sharply.

"I . . . came here a couple of nights after we met," Chloe admitted. "Your door was open and I found you lying on the floor, all . . . suffocating and covered in hives and stuff. I called 911."

"That was *you?* I would have died if you hadn't come. I was all alone here." He shivered. It was weird seeing the sexy guy from the club—the one she almost had sex with. "They said I was in shock, the whole deal. My body just started attacking itself and they couldn't figure out why."

"But they were able to treat you," she said, again neutrally, trying to sound like she wasn't digging for information.

He shook his head, his beautiful black hair staying neatly put. "They couldn't do anything. I went into a coma . . . and then one day I just suddenly got better. I woke up and it was all over. They said it was like my body was all of sudden able to heal itself or something. No explanation. I just woke up, on October 19."

"Well, I'm glad you're okay. I just came back to see how you were." Chloe turned to go, feeling it was a good time to exit.

He put a hand out to stop her. "But they said no one was in the apartment when the ambulance came."

"I freaked and ran away. Sorry about that," Chloe apologized with a small smile. Why was it easier to tell a stranger the whole truth than her friends and family? "If my mom found out I was in some strange guy's apartment at night—even if it wound up saving his life—*my* life would be over."

Xavier laughed, an open, clear-eyed laugh that held none of the seducer's smile from the night at the club.

"In fact, I should probably get going," she added. *Okay, you're not dead. This is where the Xavier-Chloe story ends. Goodbye and good luck. No more complications.* "Like I said, I just wanted to make sure you were okay."

"I mean it, I owe you, Chloe," he said standing up with her, wiping his mouth with the back of his hand in an extremely sexy, masculine way. "I would have died. If there's anything you want or need, name it. Even, like, help moving in somewhere," he added with a grin of teeth as white as the plastered wall on the postcard of Santorini that hung on Chloe's fridge.

"Uh, I'll keep that in mind." Although the idea of a

rich young Euro playboy who owed her was an intriguing concept—visions of a free vacation in Greece came to mind—Chloe was pretty sure she was never going to see him again.

"Hey," he called as she walked out. "Maybe I'll see you at The Bank sometime?"

"Maybe!" Chloe shouted back. But she was already two flights down.

Nine

Xavier was alive.

Chloe repeated this over and over to herself as she rode the bus to Sausalito, her foot impatiently marking the seconds as she tapped it against the seat in front of her.

There still remained the mystery of how he "just woke up," but it seemed like her kiss wasn't fatal—this time, at least. Maybe it wouldn't be for Brian either. Maybe the curse was losing its power as the centuries wore on, remaining overhyped as something to scare the kids with. Maybe everything was going to be okay.

A bubble of hope grew out of control in the back of Chloe's head, threatening to explode and drench her spirit with joy. She tried to rein it in, not wanting to be disappointed later if reality went south on her. Instead she channeled it into movement, leaping off the bus as soon as it stopped and running all the way to Firebird.

No going in the back way this time. Chloe was the *leader of this Pride,* for chrissake. She didn't need to go slinking around into her own den, embarrassed by the presence of her human boyfriend and intimidated by Sergei. Chloe walked right up to the front door and strode in breezily past the receptionist.

"I'll tell Sergei you are in," the sharp-angled woman said with the slightest of bows.

"Tell him I'll be right there," Chloe said, trying not to snap, not looking over her shoulder. "There's something I have to do."

How did a leader speak to her subjects? Not that she was, really—but she wasn't going to be treated as a helpless teenage girl by Sergei and his employees anymore. Until she found a middle ground, it was going to be tricky.

And as much as she wanted—*needed*—to see Brian, there was another person Chloe had to talk to first.

She went straight to the sanctuary, knocking on the door lightly before cracking it open and stepping silently in. Surprisingly, Kim wasn't there, though the lingering traces of incense indicated her recent presence. There was another Mai woman there—Valerie, Igor's fiancée. She was bent over on the floor before the statues of the twins Bastet and Sekhmet, murmuring something plaintively. She was beautiful, a perfect devoted servant of the Twin Goddesses, and might have been taken right off an Egyptian wall painting had it not been for her bright lavender suit and stiletto heels.

Chloe backed up quietly until she was out, not clicking

the door completely closed, afraid of disturbing the woman. What was she praying for? Her marriage? A baby? Or was her visit just something routine—like going to mass every Sunday? Chloe wasn't sure she could show that much devotion to the goddesses she supposedly received her power from; in the same way that Buddhism sounded neat, she was just too Western, Judeo-Christian monotheistically raised to be able to treat ancient deities with much belief or reverence.

Valerie had taken down a deer with her bare hands— and claws—on the Hunt that Chloe had attended. Another thing Chloe was also pretty sure she couldn't do. *They should have chosen* her, she thought sadly. *Or Kim.* People who actually deserved leadership of the Mai.

She headed upstairs to the library, the other obvious place Kim would be, though she checked the dining room and the little Firebird kitchenette first. All empty. *Except for the usual coffee-swilling real estate drones.*

Chloe kicked herself mentally. A lot of these people would have died for an opportunity to live in America and be—mostly—left alone with their Mai habits to work for a Mai company and be fairly well paid to do so. She would really have to stop judging people so much if she was actually going to be a leader.

Bingo.

Her friend stood at the end of a long bookshelf, silently turning the pages of a monstrous leather-bound volume. The long windows were shaded and draped by equally long velvet curtains; motes of dust hung silently in the air, unsparkled by any stray beam of sun. It was to protect the ancient and rare books, Chloe understood, but the darkness made the whole place also kind of reek of doom.

Kim looked up directly at her, even though Chloe could have sworn she hadn't made any noise.

"Hello," the girl with the black, velvety cat ears said in a normal voice, strangely out of place in a room that demanded whispering.

"Hey, Kim—I have a question for you."

Kim's ears flicked back and her green slit eyes focused, waiting.

"Is there a chance . . ." Chloe bit her lip. She was calling into question all this other girl believed in. She sucked it up. "Is there a chance that the whole human-and-Mai curse thing could be a little, well, overblown?"

Kim blinked her heavy eyelashes. "Which part? The feud? The story of the Mai girl who was killed?"

"No, the, uh, biological particulars. Could it be a complete fib that humans and Mai can't interact?"

"Chloe, unlike many of the Mai, I believe that you are free to choose your relationships however you wish, but I cannot advise testing that theory on any human you particularly like."

"No, no." Chloe sighed and sat down on the edge of a table—something she would have been screamed at for in any other library in the world. Kim merely raised an eyebrow. Chloe couldn't help noticing the Ethernet ports and wireless broadband antennas that stuck out of the center of the table, incongruous against the old wood and tarnished brass printers' lamps. The Mai were such a strange mix of boldly going modern and completely hung up on the past. "Look, I've already kissed two humans—uh, boys."

Kim's eyebrows climbed even higher than Dr. Lovsky's had. "The one at the club . . . Olga mentioned it," Kim said.

"Yeah, I checked up on him. He's *fine* now."

Kim stood in way that implied that had she a tail, it would have been swishing back and forth. "And who else? Paul, maybe?"

Chloe started. "What? I don't know, maybe as a kid. No, I meant *Brian*. Right before he conked out." Didn't Kim realize how much she liked him? And what did Paul have to do with anything? "And Dr. Lovsky says he's recovering normally."

The two girls looked at each other for a long moment.

"It sounds like our curse is somehow being lifted or fading," Kim said slowly, thinking. "How exactly did the boy from the club 'recover'?"

"I don't know. He said he just sort of woke up; they told him that he suddenly just 'got better.'"

"And when exactly did this happen?"

"Uh, October 19th."

Kim's eyes widened. "That's the night you died—at the Presidio, with everyone."

"Yeah, so . . . ?" Chloe hadn't made the connection and still didn't see what it had to do with anything.

"You're lifting the curse!" her friend practically shouted, scaring Chloe with her intensity.

"Um . . . what?"

"You died *saving a human!*"

"She's my *mom,* Kim. . . ."

"Yes, but listen—we were cursed because we killed whole villages of humans!" Kim said excitedly, her fangs gleaming and her eyes a little crazy. "Maybe because you died saving one, it mitigates our burden. And Brian? How is he?"

"I'm going downstairs to see him now, but the doctor said that so far he hasn't shown any signs of anything."

Kim glowed with excitement. "I must research this further," she said, disappearing back into the stacks. "I'll call you later if I find an answer!"

As she headed downstairs to the hospital room, Chloe smiled to herself at the idea of *her* lifting an ancient curse. Besides it meaning that everyone would be okay . . . how cool was that? It finally sounded like something a real leader would do.

Brian was still unconscious on the bed, IVs and tubes sticking in and out of his body. There was almost

114

no discernable change from the other day, except that maybe his wounds looked a little scabbier, like they were beginning to heal around the edges. Maybe. No signs of death or toxic shock.

"Hey," Chloe said softly, taking his hand. Without her realizing it, her claws came out, slowly and delicately. She used them to comb back his hair.

"Oh." Dr. Lovsky stopped short when she came in and saw the two of them together. "I, uh, I'll just leave the two of you alone. . . ."

"No, it's okay. Has he shown any signs of—has he—?" Chloe didn't know how to say it.

"There has been no sign of any of the traditional symptoms associated with humans who have . . . closely interacted with Mai," the doctor answered, shaking her head. "I even went back and looked up in our oldest documents any description of what happens. Boils. Fever. Strange bruises and scratches." She ticked them off on her clawed fingers. "Inability to breathe. Eyes sealed shut. Blood from the pores. *Nothing.* Zero. Zip. Nada. Aside from being severely beaten, Brian is fine."

Chloe's bubble of hope grew a little bigger.

"I don't understand it at all. I'm completely thrilled for my patient, but . . . I've *seen* what happens when a Mai kisses a human," Dr. Lovsky said helplessly. "Anyway, the best thing for him now is rest—and lots of antibiotics—to let his body get on with the process of healing."

"Why antibiotics?"

Dr. Lovsky narrowed her eyes at Chloe as if she were an idiot and raised one eyebrow to further illustrate her feelings. "You *found* him *injured* on the *street* in a *puddle*. Would you like me to list all the sorts of buggies an already-stressed body can be taken up with?"

"Uh, no, that's okay," Chloe said, quickly holding up her hand. "I get it. Thanks for everything."

Dr. Lovsky left and Chloe turned back to Brian.

He rustled in the bedclothes—though his leg in the cast was eerily still. "Chloe?" he whispered hoarsely.

"I'm here," she whispered back, kissing his cheek as lightly as possible. While it might not have mattered, there was no reason to tempt the Fates.

"Where am I?" After a few tries he managed to open his crusted eyes. Chloe swallowed her sadness at the damage done to another human being, the ravaging of his good looks. Brian's eyes were red and there was a pool of blood or something covering half of his left one; his right was sunk in a swollen mass of purple flesh.

What a stupid, stupid *thing!* was all she could think.

"You're safe," she said, deciding that was the easiest answer.

He snorted. Then he coughed, a long, rasping fit.

"No," he croaked. "Really." His dull eyes managed to twinkle just a little.

Chloe sighed.

"You're in the emergency room of Mai HQ. Can't reveal the location; it's a secret."

"I'm—" He hacked some more. Spittle came out of his mouth and ran down his chin. No blood this time, Chloe was relieved to see. Before she even thought about it, she took the edge of her shirt and wiped his face with it. "I'm *where?*"

"Well, where *else* was I supposed to take you?" she snapped with feigned annoyance. She was just relieved he was able to speak this coherently.

"That doctor . . . lady . . . ?" A weak finger pointed at the door.

"Mai."

Brian took so long to answer that she was afraid he had fallen asleep with his eyes open.

"Holy crap," he finally said, groaning. "Irony . . ."

"Shhh. Rest."

"Not . . . dead . . ." he suddenly realized, eyes flaring. He turned his head and tried to move his shoulders so he could look at her. "I *kissed* you! Not dead . . . How?"

Chloe shook her head. "I don't know. . . . Kim thinks the curse might be lifting because I saved a human life—my mom's." She decided *not* to burden him, once again, with the details of Xavier. Later. When he was feeling better.

"Kiss me," he ordered.

So she did.

He pulled her partly onto the bed with him, and except for one bad moment when her elbow dug into what was probably a cracked rib, they remained that way for a while. . . .

Chloe was so distracted by the fact that Kim seemed to be right—the curse did seem to be lifted—that when she finally left to go see Sergei, she forgot to be nervous or worried.

"Hey," she said. Olga and Sergei were bent over his desk together, looking at a newspaper or a contract or something. Her short platinum hair and his natural tweedy orange clashed so badly that Chloe almost had to look away.

When Olga looked up and saw her, she smiled with genuine affection and dipped her head.

"Yes, Chloe." Sergei also smiled, but Chloe saw something else in his blue-water eyes: fear, mistrust, eagerness; she couldn't tell. "Oh, and we're confirmed for Tuesday, October 28. Your introduction to the Pride."

"Oh, great. I have to check my class schedule and talk with Mom, but I don't see why not." All Chloe could picture was Sergei onstage in a giant auditorium, speaking at a blue-draped podium with Chloe sitting in a folding chair beside him, waiting to be introduced. All of the eyes she could see beyond the foot- and spotlights were slit, and there were occasional hisses from the audience.

"Has Kim fitted you with a robe yet?" Olga asked, jotting something down on the PalmPilot she carried.

If only that woman knew how ridiculous those words sounded coming out of her mouth. Chloe could just see it on her college application: Math team, AP French, and two years of mostly dead ancient-Egyptian-related language and religion. Well, at least Brown would be interested.

"Robe?"

"You have to start learning the Precepts of the Mai and at least some of our language before the ritual."

"Ritual?" The scene in Chloe's head switched from a high-school assembly to a cross between a bat mitzvah and something she might have seen on *Buffy*.

"Chloe, you have to start taking this seriously," Sergei said sternly. "It is not all about fun and power."

She opened her mouth to tell him Kim's theory about the curse and her possible lifting of it—but something made her stop. Something her cat-eared friend had told her weeks ago, when she first came to the mansion, about not always revealing everything she knew.

Sergei misinterpreted the look in her eyes and sighed. "I'm just trying. . . . There's a lot more to being a leader than just, well, 'leading,' Chloe. You really need to understand the soul of our people. And while you were born with a better *natural* insight of our ways and religion, you are still without a connection to those who live it every day."

"Yeah, I know, you're right," Chloe admitted.

"Even those of us who have had many years of experience can still make horrible mistakes. . . . I feel terrible about what happened to your mother, Chloe," he said out of nowhere and stiffly, as if he wasn't used to apologizing. "My previous decision to not risk Mai life for the mother of the Chosen—of *any* Mai—was shortsighted and foolish and almost led to great harm. Anything

119

could have happened once the Order kidnapped her—and I would have been partially to blame."

Where is he going with this? Chloe wondered.

"I know how important your human friends and family are to you. At least I do now." He tapped a manila folder on his desk. "Consider this a peace offering, not a bribe. I've set our human resources department the task of finding your adoptive father."

Of all the things Chloe was expecting him to say, this definitely wasn't one of them. She felt like she had been hit on the forehead with a shovel, too stunned to speak.

"My dad?" She stared at the folder, wanting and not wanting to reach for it.

"We don't have anything yet," Olga said gently. "But we've tackled tougher cases—nameless orphan Mai half a world away. We will find him," she added.

"Oh." Chloe shifted her weight from one foot to another. "Thanks." She got up and turned to leave, unsure what else to do. "I guess I'll see you. . . ."

"Chloe—," Sergei called. She looked back. He had a pained expression on his face, like he was really trying to get through to her but didn't know how. "Olga and I are here for you, for whatever you need. *Anything.*"

"Thanks," Chloe said, maybe actually meaning it this time.

She closed the door behind her and stood there a moment in the lobby, trying to take in what had just happened. He was going to help find her dad. Her *human* dad. It was obviously Sergei's way of apologizing.

"Honored One," Igor greeted her coldly, approaching Sergei's office. His eyes never looked more feline as the light caught his irises and made them almost red.

"Igor," Chloe said uncomfortably.

There was no trace of the former friendliness he had shown her when she had interned briefly at Firebird. "I heard about the big meeting—where you will take over," he hissed. "Sergei has devoted his *entire life* to the Pride, you know."

So much for automatic acceptance of their divinely gifted spiritual leader, she thought glumly. There didn't seem to be an upside to any of this.

"I'm not trying to take it away from him. This is the way I was *born*," Chloe said, a little desperately.

"Yes. Just remember, while you were being raised by *humans,* Sergei was helping to save the *Mai.*" And he strode off—*Rather cowardly,* Chloe thought—not giving her a chance to reply.

"This just keeps getting better and better," she muttered.

Things seemed to be finally getting back to normal that evening. After homework, Chloe treated herself to watching some dorky reality show and flipping through the latest *Vogue.* It was the first mindless, enjoyable downtime she'd had in weeks.

"Hey." Her mom suddenly appeared next to her, kneeling by the couch with an expectant look on her face. For the second time that day Chloe was pretty sure she didn't like where things were about to go.

"Yeah?" Chloe said suspiciously.

"I was just thinking about Paul and Amy, and you and all the stress you're under, and your, uh, other friends . . . Alyec, and the one with the ears. . . ."

"Yes?" Chloe said, still suspicious.

"Well." Her mother brushed a wispy lock of ash blond hair behind her ear, once again pixie perfect. Her earrings—replacements for the ones she'd dropped at the Order's hideout when she was kidnapped—swung, hypnotic dark silver crescent pendulums. "Whatever happens, I really need to be more informed about your life and get to know your friends better." While this was said lightly, there was a look in Anna King's eyes that allowed no defiance. This was a Mother Decision.

Chloe braced herself.

"I was thinking about throwing a little pizza party for all of you," her mom said with a brilliantly white grin.

The surprise party that she had thrown for Chloe's sixteenth birthday was actually pretty swank and fun. But this . . .

"Awww, Mom! Come *on*," Chloe said desperately. "That was cool when I was, like, *ten*. . . ."

"It's still fun," her mom insisted. "We can do make-your-own pizzas—maybe even get the dough from

Carlucci's. Different toppings—it will be totally retro. Like a little pre-Halloween party."

"This is *not* a good idea," Chloe pleaded.

"I'd really like to meet your friends," her mom said through gritted teeth. "Since they came to help rescue you and me."

"You know how, like, *Angel* and *Buffy* used to do crossovers? Like, Willow showing up on *Angel* and Angel appearing in the last episode of *Buffy?*" Chloe said, trying not to sound whiny. "Well, *Smallville* and *The O.C.* don't—and this is like that. Paul and Amy are breaking up. Amy and Alyec . . . something weird is going on there. And *Kim?* Mom, you don't even know her—she's a freak. I love her, but she's not exactly a party animal and she doesn't like Alyec, either. . . . I just can't really deal with this whole worlds-colliding idea."

"I want. To meet. Your friends."

The Mai had a thing or two to learn about intimidation from this woman who had normal, round pupils, Chloe decided.

She sank woefully back into the couch. No good could come of this.

Ten

"Hello, Mrs. King."

Chloe's mom opened the door for Kim, then stared at her. She wore a black felt hat pulled tightly down to cover her ears and loose black jeans with a frumpy black sweater, like she was trying to disguise her whole body, not just her head. Round Lennon-style sunglasses with thick red lenses hid her slitted eyes. She stuck a *gloved* hand out and presented Anna King with a bouquet of flowers. "Here. I hope this is an acceptable hostess gift. Thank you for inviting me to the party. I've never been to one before."

Chloe closed her eyes in horror and exhaustion. Amy tried not to giggle, for the first time ever not the weirdest and most socially inept person at a party.

"You can take all that off," Chloe said, trying to sound lighthearted and polite. "Mom saw you at the Presidio, and anyway, she knows who you are."

"These are *lovely* flowers, Kim, thank you." Chloe's

mom had her game face on, but she was genuinely touched by the gesture. She rummaged for just the right vase in the cabinets. Kim took off her gloves distastefully and removed her hat.

"Here, I think this will do." Anna King turned around with the flowers nicely arranged in a cobalt blue crystal thing just in time to see Kim running her clawed hands through her hair, scratching at the base of her unfolding, velvet black ears. "Ah," she said, trying not to look surprised, trying desperately for the politically correct you-can't-shock-me look she usually reserved for transsexuals or the severely deformed.

"I've never interacted with humans like this before—undressed, I mean," Kim said, a little uncomfortably.

"Hey, have a drink," Amy suggested, waving at a little platter of virgin coladas with grenadine "blood" dripping down the sides of the glasses. Sometimes Chloe wished she had a younger sister just so her mom would have someone else to get all Martha Stewart on.

Kim picked up a plastic glass suspiciously and her tongue darted out, taking the smallest lick from the top. Apparently it was acceptable; her eyes widened and she took a sip.

"He's such a douche bag," Amy said, turning to Chloe and continuing their conversation from before as if nothing had happened. Kim nodded wisely as if she knew what was going on. "He just fucking gave back the CDs I gave him, like I was just loaning them or something. 'Oh, uh, Amy, I think these are yours,'" Amy said, standing on her toes and imitating him. "What's up with *that?*"

"Paul and Amy are definitely breaking up," Chloe told Kim, feeling the need to let her in on it. Also, it gave her something else to do. It was easy to console Amy when the boy involved was someone Chloe barely knew; with previous boyfriends she had joined in with a happy chorus of "he can go to hell" and wishing various poxes on his genitalia.

She didn't really want to say anything bad about Paul—although he really *was* being a douche about this, Chloe reflected. But he had his own shit to deal with. . . . She really didn't know *what* to say or do now.

"Is this a bad thing?" Kim asked with all the innocence of a vaguely interested psychotherapist.

"He . . . I . . . ," Amy began and stopped. "He's just being a total douche bag about it!"

"Do you want to stay together?" Kim said, in a tone that was like she was just repeating the previous question.

"I don't know. Not if he's going to be like this all the time."

Chloe marveled at how well Amy and Kim seemed to be getting along. They seemed to have bonded even more since the night at the diner; Amy was spilling her guts to the girl she normally would have been dead jealous of—beautiful, exotic, and far more outré than herself. "I don't know *how* to break up," Amy finally admitted, pulling one of her dark locks straight. "I don't know if we can go back—if *I* can go back to just being friends again." She paused, chewing her lip uncertainly. "We were intimate, you know? We—"

"Stop," Chloe suggested, deciding it was time she entered the conversation again. "Please."

The three of them were silent, sipping their drinks for a moment.

"He wasn't very good," Amy couldn't help saying.

"Stop," both Kim and Chloe said at the same time.

"Your necklace," Kim began, trying to change the conversation, "is fascinating—it's one of our Twin Goddesses."

"Bastet, yeah. What do you mean Twin Goddesses?" Amy asked, fingering the little cat charm she had worn every day since her bat mitzvah.

"Bastet and Sekhmet, the goddesses of the Mai. Whose divine blood runs in our veins and whom we worship."

"Get out!" Amy said, excited. "You all are like *Egyptian* and polytheistic and stuff?"

Chloe shook her head as the two girls spoke animatedly about religion. *Even Amy would make a better Mai priestess than me.* Aside from being Jewish, her best friend was always the one into Wicca stuff, and Buddhism, and ancient pantheons and things like that.

Just when Chloe began to relax, Paul and Alyec

arrived—together. Which was weird for a number of reasons, not the least of which that the latter had been dissing the former pretty badly just a couple of days before.

"Hey, Mrs. King," Paul said. He came bearing a Greek salad.

"Nice to meet you, Chloe's mom," Alyec said, both charming and breezy, polite and insouciant. *That's Alyec.* She hadn't really talked to her mom much about him or Brian since being caught dating both of them—when she wasn't originally allowed to date anyone at all. That would require talking about Brian, and that was still a subject best left alone until he had fully recovered.

Alyec also brought her mom flowers but presented them with more of a flourish than Kim. Once again Chloe wondered if some of the stranger habits of her new family were a result of being Mai or Eastern European.

"*Two* bouquets in one day," her mom said, instantly smitten with Alyec like every other female on the planet. "I haven't gotten that many even on Valentine's Day."

"Chloe." Alyec came over and kissed her on the cheek, a safe bet. Paul and her mom exchanged pleasantries, then Paul suddenly found himself deeply interested in a bowl of wasabi peas.

"Hey," Chloe said uncertainly.

"I'm sorry—," Alyec began. Somehow she suspected it was something he wasn't used to saying.

"No, you're completely right," Chloe said, stopping him. "I . . . wasn't treating you fairly."

Amy had discreetly removed herself a few feet, look-ing at their CD collection, eventually wandering over to Paul. Chloe's mom had managed to corner Kim and was questioning her as politely as she could without reverting to lawyer mode.

"So, you've lived with your, uh, *Pride* your entire life?" her mom was asking Kim interestedly, popping a chip into her mouth. "Never went to school or anything?"

It was supposed to sound neutral, a casual question, like Anna King was talking to another adult. But Chloe could hear the tone in her voice, see the look on her face: maternal concern was beginning to manifest. Chloe thought about her biological sister, the one whom she had only found out about recently, the one who had been murdered—probably by the Rogue—before they ever had a chance to meet. She had told her mom about the other Mai girl but wondered what would happen if she had brought her home. What would Anna King do?

Throw a party, came the obvious answer.

"So," Amy said, turning back to Alyec. "How's the music for the prom coming along, prom boy?"

She cocked her head and sat down. Amy's latest new look involved shorts almost like knickers, tights, leg warmers, and a cardigan over a T-shirt on top. Long used to looking at the outfits while carefully erasing her friend from the picture, Chloe could see it was a look that might actually grace a runway. Amy, while pretty in her own way, never really made a good model for the clothes she designed. Her looks were complicated, second-look beauty; she should have worn simpler outfits.

And if Chloe didn't know better, she would have thought Amy was interacting almost humanly with Alyec for once.

"It's not a prom," Alyec said haughtily. "It's a *fall formal*. And *I* managed to help snag Xtian Blu to spin for an hour."

"No *way!*" Paul said, his jaw dropping as he joined the conversation.

"Yep," Alyec said smugly. Amy and Chloe rolled their eyes, having no idea who the DJ was.

"Doesn't anyone ever hire bands anymore?" Chloe's mom asked plaintively. "Even jazz?"

"Who played at your prom?" Paul asked politely.

"Formal," Alyec corrected.

Anna King sighed in happy memory. "The Creepy Sheep."

Chloe wasn't the only one staring at her. Even Kim's eyes widened. "It was the seventies. It was *punk*," Anna protested.

"This is a dance?" Kim asked. She finished her virgin colada down to its dregs, sticking her inhumanly long and narrow tongue into the core to scrape up the bits. Her fangy canines made little clicking noises against the glass. Chloe's mom tried not to stare.

"The theme is 'Something Wicked This Way Comes,' Mrs. King," Alyec said, not really answering her. "We're getting a drama geek to do the lighting—make it look all like trees and stuff. The disco ball," he said with great wisdom, "is the *moon.*"

"Are all the DJ slots filled?" Paul asked casually, tracing the lip of his cup. Still full, Chloe noted, of virgin colada-y goodness.

"There's still nine to ten, for people who show up early. Do you want to take it?"

"Sure," he said, trying not to grin.

"I've never been to a dance before," Kim said, to no one in particular.

The comment hung in the air. Even Chloe's mom seemed like an awkward teenager, not knowing what to say.

"Is it fun?" she demanded.

"No . . ."

"Not really . . ."

"They're actually kind of a drag."

"Totally boring . . ."

"But you're all going," Kim noted.

Again the silence.

"You." Paul coughed. "You, uh, want to go?"

"I'd love to. Thanks," Kim said promptly. She tried to make it sound as toneless as everything else, but she couldn't hide the delight in her face.

"Uh, 'scuse me, I gotta go use the euphemism," Chloe said, trying to cover her giggles.

Alyec extended his hand with a little flourish to help her out of the deep couch. She took it and pulled herself up, as effortlessly and gracefully as someone who wasn't human. Someone Mai. Alyec showed no strain or effort; the tips of his fingers barely moved. For some reason, this little thing, this private moment that took less than five seconds to pass imprinted itself with crystal permanence in Chloe's mind. *She was not human. He was not human.* According to ancient myth, they could not have sex with humans—only each other. The rest of the Pride already approved of the Chosen and Alyec as a lifelong couple.

Tears sprang to her eyes.

"I don't *want* this," she whispered, then headed for the bathroom, already crying.

"I'll go check on her," Alyec said before Amy could. Their voices were muffled through the door—which she slammed shut. The cool tiles and porcelain in the bathroom were overwhelmingly appealing; Chloe sat down on the side of the tub and put her head in her hands.

"Chloe?" Alyec knocked lightly on the door with his knuckle. "Are you . . . okay?"

She began to sob, rocking back and forth.

"Chloe," Alyec said softly, opening the door and sitting down next to her.

"I don't want, I mean, I want"—she tried to say in between tears—"I want my *old* life again. I want my friends acting normal. I want my mom acting normal—this party is the craziest thing she's done yet. *I don't want to be leader of the Pride,*" she cried viciously. "I *don't.* It's not *fair.* They expect me to just pick up and rotate my life a full one-eighty—to stop being a high-school student and start leading them into glory."

"No one thinks—," Alyec began.

"Yes, they *do-oo!*" Chloe sobbed. "Everyone keeps saying I can have a normal life and go to Berkeley or whatever, but I have to do all these other things—rituals and stuff I don't even believe in. I can't lead anyone. I can't lead myself. I *suck.*" It all came out, loud. Everything that had been growing in the back of her head, whispered cynicisms and sly doubts, finally burst forth. "I've been mean to you, I don't deserve you, you shouldn't be here. . . ."

"You're not mean to me," Alyec said softly, with a faint smile. "You may be confused about a lot of things right now, Chloe King, but I can tell you that you are not *mean.* Except maybe to yourself."

Chloe kept crying.

"I want to start the year over," she moaned. "I want—this all—to stop."

"Shhh." Alyec finally put his arms around Chloe and began to rock her.

"Paul is taking Kim to the prom—*dance,* excuse me. Amy obviously wants to go with you. She totally does. Brian can't go because he's sort of almost dead. I couldn't go anyway because I'm going to be *really* busy learning dead languages and leading the Pride and being on the math team and it's not like I'm even part of *high* school anymore. . . ."

She wiped her face with the back of her hand, eyes burning from the tears and nose definitely swollen. *I probably look like shit.* But most of the crying seemed to be over; Chloe was just angry.

"It must be really confusing for you right now," Alyec said, giving her shoulders a squeeze. "I wish I could help."

"Mai relationships are a lot less . . . *complicated* than human ones, aren't they?" she asked, sighing.

"I think they're a lot more *immediate,*" Alyec said with a grin. "Instead of getting upset or running away, if you had been raised Mai and didn't like seeing me with Amy, you probably would have let your claws out."

Chloe smiled a little at that.

"I like that you care enough to be jealous," he said gently, squeezing her arm. They sat quietly for a few minutes, Chloe resting her head up against his shoulder.

It was nice, but if she was going to lead anyone anywhere, it had to begin with the truth. *And here's a good place to start.*

"Alyec, I think . . ." She took a deep breath. "I don't think this is exactly what I want right now."

He looked a little upset but nodded. "I've been a little freaked out since the whole thing about marriages in the library. . . ." He struggled for words. "It's a lot of pressure, and to be suddenly dating the One . . ." He trailed off for a second. "It's not that I don't think someday, maybe—and this wasn't just all fun or anything—I didn't think at the beginning anyone would be looking at it to be permanent. We're *dating,* for chrissake. One thing about the Mai . . . our options for even dating are limited," he said a little sadly.

To her embarrassment, Chloe hadn't thought about any of this from his perspective before; suddenly he wasn't just fooling around with a new member of their community—he was going out with the Chosen One. In a lot of the older people's minds they were probably already engaged, with children, and leading the Mai together into a whole new era of peace and prosperity. She breathed a deep sigh of relief and held herself back from telling him that the curse might be lifting and that maybe they really could date other people—it just didn't seem like the right time.

Paul's favorite episode of *Star Trek* came to her mind: *"I found I did not wish to be married to a legend. . . ."*

Alyec as her consort. It just didn't work.

"Is there anything else you want to get off your chest?" Alyec asked gently.

"Let's see," Chloe said, wiping the last of her tears away. "I have just been made leader to a people I know almost nothing about. People aren't exactly rooting for me, you know. I'm still behind at school, and my relationship with my mom has been all fucked up since I've, um, fully become a Mai. I don't belong anywhere, and my *friends*"— she indicated the kitchen with her thumb—"have their own things going on. Oh, *and* there's someone following me."

"What are you talking about?" Alyec asked, meaning her last point. "The Rogue is dead; you sort of forced an uneasy truce on both us *and* the Tenth Blade. And no matter what Igor or anyone who supports Sergei really thinks, no Mai would ever dare lay a hand on you."

"I just have this feeling that someone is following me—I know it. What about that guy who hates Brian? Rick or Dick or whatever, who was with Whitney Rezza the night at the Presidio . . ."

"I hardly think he could sneak up on *you;* he's just a human and not even as good as the Rogue."

The streetlamp outside glowed through the frosted window, making everything in the bathroom bleak and soft at the same time, well defined but gray. Individual tiles stood out against old grout; larger things like the mirror and the sink seemed to fade into a matte painting of a bathroom. A car went by, breaking the silence for a few moments.

"Do you know who tried to kill Brian?" Alyec asked softly.

"No, I haven't asked." She pulled some toilet paper off the roll, wadded it up, and daubed her nose. "I guess I should."

"I wouldn't worry too much." He put his hands around her shoulders and gave her a squeeze. "You can take on whatever they dish out," he added, brushing her cheek with his hand and pushing back a stray lock of her dark hair. "Why don't we go back to the party?"

She nodded, sniffing. He tore off some toilet paper

for her to blow her nose on and they returned to the living room, Chloe hoping desperately she didn't look like an idiot.

"Everything okay?" Amy murmured.

"Yep," Chloe said, wiping her nose again and knowing what a liar her red and puffy face made her out to be. Kim looked alarmed. "I just—I had a little bit of a breakdown."

Her mother was stationed behind the kitchen island, clasping the sides like it was the wheel of a ship. Her knuckles were white.

"I'm, uh, a little overstressed right now," she added with faint smile. "It just kind of all got to me."

Chloe felt like she was eleven again, when she'd run to her room crying during her birthday party. All the boys had decided to play football in the street and Jason Pellerin told her that *she* couldn't because she was in a dress. Chloe had stayed in her room a good long time, weeping. By the time she finally came out, the party was sort of stilted and over.

"You know what you need?" Paul asked, breaking the silence. *"Marriage wanna."*

"Paul," her mom said warningly.

"How about a *Matrix* marathon?" Amy asked, digging through her voluminous pink purse, whose trim matched the fringe on her leg warmers. "I was just going to lend these to someone. . . ."

"That sounds . . . *excellent*," Chloe said, breathing a

deep sigh of relief. Suddenly the whole tension of the party was broken. *TV—the ultimate party solution.* Paul and Alyec were obviously interested, and Kim took the DVDs, turning them over curiously in her hand. Her mother went back to chopping pepperoni.

"I've never actually seen the third one," she said, without looking up from her cutting board and chef's knife.

"It *sucked*," Alyec, Paul, Amy, and Chloe all said at the same time.

"Like the dance," Kim said wryly. "And like the dance, we are going to watch it anyway."

"*Now* you're getting it," Paul said, clapping her on the back.

Chloe wiped her face but wasn't embarrassed about it anymore. The boys took over the seemingly difficult process of putting in the DVDs and setting up the TV, and Amy made kettle corn in the microwave.

"Are you feeling better?" Kim asked quietly.

Chloe nodded and smiled. "I just needed to—I needed the cry." Waves of endorphins and relief were still washing over her. Like it was all going to be all right now. "What did you all do while I was gone?"

"Not much," Kim admitted. "I thought I heard someone approaching the house; that was exciting for a moment. But no one was there."

Chloe felt her waves break. But before she could question her further, Kim turned abruptly to Paul. "Are you going to drink that?" she asked, pointing to his glass.

"Huh?" Paul reluctantly dragged his attention away from wide-screen and Dolby digital options. Alyec grabbed the remote while he looked, distracted, at his still-full but slowly melting virgin colada. "Um, well." He looked at Chloe's mom, trying to decide what to do. "No," he finally said.

Kim reached over and took it with both hands, then began lapping at it greedily. "This," she pronounced, licking the slightest bit of foam off her lips, "is a good party."

Eleven

It will be *okay,* Chloe told herself the next morning, sort of believing it this time. Her mom seemed satisfied—or possibly horrified—and likely to drop the whole needing-to-be-more-in-her-life thing for a while. After sitting through all six hours of the *Matrix* with Amy snoring through the first hour of *Revolutions,* Kim pausing the videos every few minutes to ask questions, and Alyec and Paul fighting during the middle of *Reloaded* about why Jet Li didn't wind up being in it, Chloe's mom was feeling pretty well acquainted with her friends.

And her Mai friends were apparently not outside the range of normal teenage behavior; even Kim with her ears and slit eyes and claws.

"She's a little bit of a geek," was all her mom had said about her after the guests had gone.

Chloe had laughed. "Yeah, the Mai think so, too."

And now here she was, a normal high-school girl

going to high school. She was almost caught up with her homework and exams and had sorted stuff out with Alyec, and Brian was recovering. It even looked like she and Brian could hook up without fatal consequences. Amy and Paul—well, they weren't really her problem. After last night her two best friends seemed to realize the amount of stress she was under and lowered the weirdness meter a bit. No longer chanting the *I will be the cool best friend* mantra, Chloe told herself instead, *They got to work their own shit out.*

After her last makeup French quiz, Chloe was so glad it was over and confident of her grade that she signed her test with a flourish and a fleur-de-lis. She handed it in with a little bow and *merci beaucoup.* Mme. Sassoon already had her car keys in her hand. Thanks to Kim, Chloe was pretty sure she would get an A.

She checked her voice mail: two messages. One from Alyec, asking how she was doing, and one from Sergei.

"Chloe, we found something on your dad. I have to look at this property near your school." Sergei described exactly where it was and how to get there. *"It's an old theater. If you meet me there at four, we can talk."*

"Sacre bleu," Chloe muttered, snapping her phone shut. He had kept his word—he was really trying. Of course she would meet him.

Speaking of French, where *had* Kim learned to speak it so well? She had never been to France, as far as Chloe knew. Many of the Mai had never been to San Francisco

142

proper, much less Canada, much less France. *Do they dream of doing other things?* A few of the Mai had broken out, like Simone the dancer, but it was rare. It was a self-imposed ghetto. She wasn't sure how much Sergei actually had to do to keep them there.

What about her own dreams, while she was at it? Running a retail clothing empire. Would she just substitute her slavery for Sergei's; would the Mai insist on working for her?

And, uh, speaking of retail empires, remember how you promised to go see Marisol . . . ?

Chloe had been putting it off for a long time, too smothered by guilt to even think about it. Now she was finally in a good enough mood that she could force herself through it and take whatever was thrown at her, whatever she deserved. She had already chalked up her relationship with the shop owner as over, so at the worst this wouldn't change anything.

She hadn't even been by Pateena's since coming back from Firebird. Once it was her safe haven, her home away from home and school. An entirely different set of people and problems and the first real hard work she had ever had to do. There was nothing to make you appreciate the weekends more than a La-Z-Boy-sized pile of jeans that needed to have their cuffs artfully ripped. Chloe's short internship at Firebird had just been boring and strenuous.

She stood outside the windows and looked at them

for a moment. They had put up a Halloween display—probably Marisol's doing. She was far more artistic than she had much of a chance to express. One mannequin hung upside down, wearing a leather jacket, like a bat; another wore all orange, like a pumpkin. A third had earmuffs redone as ears and long black Lee Press-On Nails for claws.

A cat, Chloe realized.

Marveling at the irony, she took a deep breath and went in.

"Well, look who's back," Lania said immediately. Of course she had to be there. Of course. Chloe's quest for redemption—and subsequent humiliation—wouldn't have been complete without it. Though a menace to retail, snotty to the customers, and still not able to understand how to void a credit card sale, the girl had been allowed to work the cash register just because she was a couple of years older than Chloe. And there she was, now assistant manager.

"Coming to get your things?" Lania pressed, hands on her hips and a smug grin on her face. She looked like an afternoon cartoon—the kind that targeted girls and involved teenagers doing shallow things to each other at malls. Chloe couldn't even work up any contempt; it would have been like dissing a clown.

"Excuse me," Chloe said instead, carefully walking around her to the back.

"She don't want to talk to you!" Lania shrieked in

the fake homegirl accent she sometimes put on. Lania was from La Jolla—her parents owned a horse ranch.

Chloe took another deep breath, pausing before the metal double doors left over from when the place had been a diner. Then she pushed her way in and sat in the folding chair in front of Marisol's desk.

Marisol was on the phone. She looked over at Chloe and then stared at her, as if she didn't trust her not to steal anything.

"Baby, I gotta call you back. Something's come up. Just wait."

The little woman was older than she looked: thick, beautiful waist-long hair went a long way to making her look like an art student. But there was a hardness in her eyes and tiny wrinkles that formed around her lips when she pursed them.

Chloe cleared her throat, suddenly not sure where to begin.

"Why did you even come back here?" the woman demanded. "To apologize? I *told* you that if you didn't show up on that Wednesday, you were gone for good. What happened, you break up with one of your two boyfriends? You get pregnant? Honey, unless someone *died,* I don't even want to hear about it."

"Well," Chloe said slowly, "a number of people actually *have* died."

Marisol's eyes widened.

Chloe thought of the Rogue and the fight at the

145

Presidio—one of the Tenth Bladers hadn't gotten up when it was over. And of course if you counted *her*, that was two deaths right there.

"My mom was kidnapped by these weird cultists. And they . . . sent this crazy serial murderer after me. And then I was sort of being held captive by these people who are kind of related to me. . . . It's kind of a long story. You can call my mom and ask her if you want, though."

There was a long moment while Marisol stared into her eyes.

"No," she finally said. "I . . . believe you." She didn't look happy, though, like she didn't *want* to believe it. She had to try one last test. "And no one missed you at school?"

"They were told I had mono. My mom's law firm was told she was on vacation."

"Are you . . . okay?"

"I'm alive." Chloe shrugged.

There was another silence between them, as Marisol was obviously trying to work out what was polite to ask about and what would be prying, what was concern and what was curiosity.

This was where Chloe could tell her. This was where she could come clean, demonstrate the claws. Show Marisol just how far from the ordinary her life had been recently; as far from work and her and vintage clothes and receipts and hems and even Lania as it could get. She *used* to tell her boss things she never would have told her mom—it was like having a much older sister or aunt with objective, slightly less "mom" views on her life.

"How are your two boyfriends?" Marisol finally asked.

The moment was over.

"Only one now. He's lying in a hospital bed recovering from having the shit kicked out of him trying to save me." Chloe decided to cut the next awkward silence short by standing up again. "Well, that's really all," she said, shrugging. "I came by to apologize and let you know that my going AWOL wasn't really without a reason."

Marisol's face softened into the look she used to have when Chloe would sometimes cry about her mom or school. "Why didn't you at least call?"

"I . . . I was feeling really guilty," Chloe admitted. But now that she thought about it, now that she was standing before the woman she was terrified of ever seeing again, it was kind of ridiculous. "You told me not to come back and all, so I figured you'd be mad at me and never want to talk to me again. You said that this was a business, not babysitting for flaky teenagers."

"Oh, Chloe, you *imbécile,*" Marisol said, smiling sadly. "I didn't know your mother was kidnapped and whatever else. I just thought you were having boyfriend problems. You could have—you *should* have called me. You should always feel you can do that, no matter what."

"Thanks," Chloe said. *Remember this,* she told herself. Not that Marisol was nice enough to forgive her, but that some things transcended personal guilt. She had to understand what was really important and what were her own screwed-up feelings and the difference between the two.

"I—I just hired this other girl," Marisol said hesitantly. "I can't give you back your old hours."

Chloe put up her hand. "Don't worry about it. Believe me, there's so much on my plate right now I'd flake on you *again,* something I'd rather avoid. And according to my biological family, I'm sort of a princess or priest or something."

Marisol looked skeptical. "Do you get a crown?"

Chloe laughed. *If only.* "No, just a whole lot of shit to learn about the people I come from."

"That doesn't sound so good. There should at least be jewels. All right, well, if you want to work some hours, call me. Andy's no worker like you. But she gets along okay with Lania."

Chloe rolled her eyes. Marisol barked with laughter.

She tried to avoid both Lania and the new girl on the way out, the latter of whom was chatting merrily on her cell phone while rearranging racks that the customers had gotten out of order. She had black goth hair, but her attitude was all wrong, kind of like a flightier version of Amy. Chloe sighed and left, unable to resist throwing one smug, calm smile in Lania's direction—the girl had obviously been trying to listen in on her and Marisol's conversation.

She wandered over to where she was supposed to

meet Sergei, correctly expecting him to be a few minutes late. Everything else about Firebird Properties ran like clockwork, but some of the older Eastern European employees, even Sergei himself, seemed to have trouble getting anywhere on time.

The theater was disappointing: there wasn't even a cool marquee or anything like that left outside, just empty frames where posters had once hung. With the ticket booth all smashed in and graffiti on its brick walls, the building looked a little *beyond* abandoned and well on its way to condemned.

If I ran Firebird, I would do something cool with this, Chloe thought. The possibilities were endless—really great apartments, an awesome bar, maybe even a theater again. For repertory movies *and* local theater, or maybe her own version of the coffeehouse in *Smallville*. Hey, Lana was like sixteen and she ran it—Chloe was sixteen, leader of her people and a cat person besides. She should have *no trouble* with just managing a coffee shop.

"Chloe."

She jumped; even without actively paying attention with her improved Mai hearing, Chloe should have been able to hear him walking up. Sergei was fairly square and . . . heavy and tended to wear shoes that clicked when he walked. But there he was, barely two feet away, a light smile on his face, hands behind his back.

He was dressed more casually than usual, and Chloe had to admit that it immediately made him a lot more likable. Even in just his polo shirt and khakis he looked less imposing, more human.

"I can't believe I startled you," he said, chuckling. "You've been living with humans for too long."

"Yeah, funny," Chloe said, instantly on the defensive again.

"Oh, I'm sorry," the older man said, instantly sighing and putting his hand to his face. "I shouldn't have said that. It's not funny. I just meant it as a joke, to lighten the tension."

Chloe relaxed a little. "I'm kind of sensitive about my mom these days."

"Completely understandable. Here, shall we go inside as we talk?" Sergei gestured for her to go first, getting a big ring of keys out of his pocket. "The fool owner couldn't meet us here; he had another prospective client for a penthouse restaurant, and this is small potatoes compared."

"That's kind of rude." Chloe was *dying* to know what Sergei found out about where her dad was or what he was up to, but she reminded herself to remain patient.

Sergei shrugged. "It's business. You have to learn, Chloe, that often nothing is personal. You can't take it to heart. You'll get ulcers. Ah, here." He found a big old-fashioned key and put it first to the locked metal bar that went through all of the metal door handles in the front. Then he took a smaller, bronze key out and opened the farthest door to the left.

"It's like a video game," Chloe ventured.

"You know, I've never played one—here, let me go first in case there's anyone in here squatting or something," he said, as if people like that were rats. He pushed his way in and shouted, *"Hellllooooooo,"* then waited to hear if there was any movement or scuttling. He nodded. "Just a whole lot of roaches. It's safe."

Chloe realized with distaste that *she* could hear the bugs, too, dozens of them, little feet making little noises as they rushed away from the light. She noticed with amusement that Sergei didn't do the thing they did in the movies, or on TV, or in real life: he didn't take out a flashlight and wave it around in the darkness, swinging its pale yellow beam over walls and doors and floors. He just walked in, waiting a moment for his eyes to adjust to almost complete darkness. If he were facing her, Chloe knew she would have seen his eyes become slits and then wide, like a cat's eyes in the dark, barely any iris showing.

The lobby didn't look all that derelict; once her own eyes adjusted, Chloe saw that the red carpet was only dusty and worn, not ripped up and moldering away. The concession counters had their glass smashed in a couple of places, and the popcorn machines were gone. A pity—she always wanted one. It would have been a fun thing to take home. There was still one napkin dispenser with napkins in it and a fake crystal chandelier that was missing some of its glass festoons and garlands.

"What are you going to do with this place?" Chloe asked, already redecorating it in her mind.

"Haven't decided yet," Sergei said, shrugging. "I know this may disappoint you, but unless the structure is really intact and we can find something to do with it, we may just raze the whole thing. The plot of land it's on is worth more for apartments. Or a parking garage—that's where the real money is."

Chloe sighed. Weren't Russians—okay, he was Abkhazian—supposed to be better educated and more artistic and intellectual than Americans? How could he miss all the decaying grandeur, the shabby beauty of this place?

"So how are you and Kim getting along with learning Mai?" he asked sort of casually, peeking over one of the counters to peer at what remained of the slushy machines.

"Uh, we haven't really started yet," Chloe admitted. "But I've just finished all my makeup work and I'm a pretty fast learner." Well, okay, that wasn't really true about languages—but she was pretty sure it was just going to be memorization. She didn't have *time* to learn all the conjugations or whatever ancient Egyptian she'd have to know for tomorrow.

"Just remember your audience," Sergei said, suggesting more than chastising. Chloe wished her mom was a little more like that sometimes. "You're kind of like a second coming to them—so you'd better not disappoint."

152

Chloe sighed again. Here it came. The second unavoidable conversation of the day. She leapt up onto the ticket taker's podium and sat there balancing on its four-inch-wide top, an impossible position for any human except maybe Jackie Chan or Jet Li.

"Sergei, I never wanted this," she admitted with all of her heart behind it. "I think I wanted to finish high school, go to college, and maybe start my own retail clothing empire. Nothing I ever wished for involved claws, paws, or leading the Mai."

"But you are who you are," Sergei said, pausing in his inspections to fix her with his slit eyes. He cocked his head like a cat. "You cannot change anything."

"What I meant was"—Chloe took a deep breath—"I don't *want* to take the Pride from you." *Unless of course it turns out that you really did send people to kill my mom.* But then Chloe would have chosen anyone else to lead besides her. Igor or Olga or someone.

"Chloe, that's very sweet," Sergei said, meaning it. "But you're not really taking it from me. You are the One, anyway—that is your right."

"Isn't it," Chloe said hesitantly, "isn't it a little weird in this day and age to have *inherited* leaders? I mean, just because I was born with certain abilities, does that really make me fit to rule?"

"It is archaic, *I* agree—even if no one else does. It's not exactly a merit-based position. I built Firebird from the ground up and love running it, but that counts for nothing. Our previous Pride Leader, everything else aside, really tried to *do* something. Her goal was to unite all of the scattered Mai in Eastern Europe, and she worked very hard to accomplish that."

Everything else aside? What did that mean?

"But Eastern Europe was—still is—a very dangerous place to be and our time there was over. Too many wars, too much prejudice, too much random violence. It was always my goal to get us out of there. To go west. Run ahead of ourselves, start over in new land. Maybe escape the old curse," he said, a little sadly. "I worked very hard to bring them here, to build Firebird, to make a safe place for all of us to live. Don't you think that makes me a leader?"

"Sure," Chloe said, not sure what else to say.

Sergei sighed. "Too bad no one else agrees with you. I wonder if there's anything actually left in the main theater—usually they tear out all the seats and sell them in auctions. After you." He opened the door for her and gave a little bow as she went in.

The darkness inside was absolute, but Chloe could feel the vastness of space around her. A good place to be scared in. She felt all floaty, like she was going to start drifting into the air.

"Hey, where are the lights?" Chloe asked.

"I'm sorry we don't have our little discussions anymore," Sergei said, his voice suddenly coming a dozen feet from her, completely unplaceable in the shadows. "And our chess games, too."

"Me too," Chloe also admitted. "Is the power out or something?" She put her hands out to find the closest wall, suddenly nervous.

"I'm going to miss having lunch with you."

"They don't have to stop just because I'm not living there anymore." Was she just being a wimp in the dark, or was there something ominous about the way he said that?

"I'm afraid that won't be possible," the older man said with regret. "Not because you're the One or anything . . ."

Suddenly all the houselights came on, full power. The theater was flooded with bright yellow light and Chloe was blinded, throwing her arms over her face a second too late.

". . . but because you'll be *dead.*"

Chloe forced her eyes open, blinking painfully as the muscles in them contracted her pupil faster and smaller than they ever had.

Before her stood the Rogue.

Twelve

The first thing she thought was, *Oh my God, he's alive.*

Alexander Smith, aka the Rogue, the psycho assassin of the Order of the Tenth Blade, should have been dead.

When Chloe fought him on the Golden Gate Bridge, she had seen him plummet to his death, or so she had thought. When the Tenth Blade found out, they sent an *army* of assassins to scour the city, looking for her to avenge his death. And the truth of the matter was, at the last minute she had extended her hand—to help *save* him, for reasons she could never really put into words more than "it seemed like the right thing to do."

He was tall, muscled, maybe a little thinner than the last time she saw him, with the same dumb white-blond ponytail over his shoulder, the same crazy eyes, the same neoprene-ish black suit that no doubt held the same innumerable daggers, blades, shuriken, and other assorted traditional weapons of the Tenth Blade.

"Chloe King," the Rogue said, with a bit of a smile.

"You're looking well," Chloe said before she could stop herself. Now was *not* the time to be funny. *And it's not like the Rogue really has a sense of humor.* "What's going on?" she demanded, swinging around to face Sergei.

"I'm . . . afraid . . . your time with us is over, Honored One," Sergei said with a little mock bow. "Sorry you'll miss the meeting tomorrow."

"Why are you doing this?" Chloe asked, knowing the answer anyway.

"Weren't you listening to *anything* I was saying?" Sergei said, exasperated. "The Pride is just going to toss me aside now that you're here. Thirty years of hard work—of my *life*—gone, just like that. I am hardly going to let a teenage upstart who was brought up with *humans* take everything away from me, whatever her lineage may be."

"Lineage . . . ?" Chloe asked, confused.

"Your mother was our previous Pride Leader." As Sergei spoke, the Rogue remained as still as a statue, only smiling occasionally at certain points. "Your sister could have been the next leader—she was older than you, you know, and required all nine blades. Had she lived, we would have had *two* 'the Ones.'" He chuckled. "That hasn't happened in a very long time."

Chloe felt something in the pit of her stomach. Imagine—a sister who could also die and come back, who could take some of this burden from her, who had been actually raised Mai and could show her the way. *Wait*—two *"the Ones"?* What about the third, the brother Kim had suggested there might be? Sergei didn't seem to know about him. . . . Chloe shoved that thought to the back of her head.

"This gentleman here"—Sergei twirled his hand at the Rogue—"took care of her. Poor girl, she shouldn't have gone wandering city streets at night by herself. . . ."

Chloe had a flash of her recurring dream—the one about her sister's death. She shuddered but refocused her attention on the present. Chloe still didn't understand. She looked back and forth between the two of them. The Rogue was *devoted* to wiping out the Mai—it was his whole life. And he and Sergei, the head of this Pride, were working *together*?

"We had tried tracking you down for a while," Sergei said, turning back to Chloe. "Finally we assumed you died in the violence between the Georgians and the Abkhazians. Imagine my surprise when you turned up *here,* right under my nose!"

"You two are working together to kill everyone who might be a real Pride Leader?"

"I really don't like that phrase," Sergei said with a pinched look. The Rogue just smiled. "But yes. For this one thing our purposes crossed paths—the Tenth Blade doesn't want any mystic, powerful leaders of the Mai who could unite them and lead them to victory—or whatever it is they think you're going to do—and I rather enjoy my current position."

"You're working with a man who wants to wipe us

out," Chloe said, the thing in her stomach becoming rage as her confusion dissipated. "With someone who has *killed* Mai! If you really love them so much, how can you murder them—us? You've told me how few there are left!" Chloe said desperately, trying to understand.

"Strange bedfellows, I know," Sergei said, nodding. "The loss of you two girls is a shame genetically, but it's a small sacrifice to prevent complete chaos in the Pride—which was working just *fine* before you came along, Miss King."

Chloe opened her mouth but didn't know what to say. The Rogue was still, but who knew how long it was going to be before he attacked? Her time was running out.

"Did you send people to kill my mother?" she finally asked quietly.

"Which one?"

Chloe's eyes narrowed. "My adoptive one." But now that she thought about it . . .

"Yes," Sergei answered promptly. "But that was before we all found out you were 'the One.' You were another Mai we welcomed into the fold, only you didn't seem to be ready yet to leave your past behind. We were just hurrying that process up a little."

"You would have had to kill more than my mom to get me into your fold completely," Chloe said hotly. "You would have had to kill Paul and Amy and Brian. . . ."

"I do what needs to be done," Sergei said, shrugging again. "Don't flatter yourself in thinking you were the first Mai to be raised by humans. There are six billion of them and only a thousand of us, Chloe. They don't need you. *We* do. Well," he added apologetically, "not *you*, obviously, but in general."

The Rogue finally seemed to be tensing a little, bored with the conversation.

"Did you even look for my dad at all?" But she already knew the answer.

Sergei put the big set of keys back in his pocket, getting ready to go. "I don't know. Olga might have since I mentioned it in front of her. I really will miss our time together," he said with a sigh. "In any other circumstances, I would be proud to be your father."

"I'm tired of listening to this," the Rogue finally growled. "Prepare to die, Mai whore." He started to cross his arms over his chest, reaching under each sleeve for a blade.

"Don't call her that," Sergei snapped, annoyed. "Just do your job."

"I'm tired of you too, Demon," the Rogue said tonelessly, and neatly whipped a shuriken at him.

Before Chloe could react, the star ended its flight buried in Sergei's throat. It stuck beneath his neat, short beard, neat, long, dark red ribbons streaming from it.

"You—," Sergei gurgled, ripping the star out of his throat. His claws came out and he launched himself at the Rogue.

Alexander leapt easily out of the way, though not so

far as to avoid one of Sergei's fat, square paws raking five bloody troughs in his arm. He spun around and buried a long knife into Sergei's back, causing him to let out something between a groan and a scream that was completely inhuman.

"You're Mai, too, Sergei Shaddar," the Rogue whispered as he held Sergei to drive the blade farther in. "You mean nothing to me."

Sergei let out a last bubbling groan and died.

Thirteen

Chloe gaped at the scene in front of her. She felt disconnected, like it was all happening on TV. There was just too much to take in.

Sergei and the Rogue had been working together. *And now the relationship seems to be, uh, over.* Sergei had helped kill her sister and lead Chloe to this theater to have the Rogue kill her, too.

Who was the better person? The assassin or the traitor to his race?

Hey, Chloe. RUN.

She shook herself out of her thoughts just as Alexander let Sergei's body drop to the floor with an ungraceful *thump*. And unlike Chloe, Sergei showed no signs of returning to life anytime soon.

"Well, what do you know," the Rogue said with little surprise, "he really wasn't the true Pride Leader."

The assassin standing before her probably knew *way* more about the Mai than she did, Chloe realized.

"Even for a Mai, he was traitorous filth," the Rogue continued, pulling out his blade and wiping it off. Then he turned to face her. "You, on the other hand . . ."

Should she stay and fight or run? The part of Chloe that had snapped her out of her thoughts before still urged the whole fleeing thing, but somehow she didn't think that would be a wise move. *No exposing the back—especially to someone who has range weapons.*

"Me, on the other hand . . . ?" she prompted, tensing, preparing herself to go into fight mode, sidestepping a few feet to the left.

"You would make a truly great leader; your false gods chose well. Too bad you're not human." He gave her a little bow. "Which is why," he added apologetically, "I *really* have to do this."

"You don't *really* have to do anything," Chloe pointed out. She moved so her back was to the theater door, Sergei's head pointing at her feet. "I've never done anything to hurt anyone—for chrissake, I even tried to save *you* from falling."

"I know." For just a moment the Rogue's cool expression broke and he looked puzzled. Then the moment was over and he gave her a grim smile, drawing out twin blades. One was still stained with Sergei's blood. "Probably comes from being raised by humans. It would be an interesting experiment—if you weren't the Chosen One, I mean—to see how you'd turn out. To see which side you'd choose."

"There. Are. No. *Sides.*" Chloe leapt just as he threw one of his long daggers at her; she went straight up and it passed beneath her to bury itself in the velvet-covered wall behind.

"There is good and evil, us and you," the Rogue said, circling to where she was, keeping his eyes locked on her.

"No, there is sane and fucking *nuts*," Chloe corrected. "Or in your case, fucking nuts and *really* fucking nuts."

At some point he had pulled out a second knife to replace the one he had thrown; Chloe was dismayed to realize she hadn't noticed it. He had also managed to force her away from the doors so they were behind her—she was now at the worst-possible angle to escape.

"And what about Brian?" she pushed, continuing clockwise around Sergei's body. His head pointed at the doors. "Was it 'good' what the Order did to him?"

The Rogue frowned. "What Richard did was inexcusable, treating a human and one of our *own* like that. There would have been other ways to deal with Whitney's son."

His hands moved so fast they blurred and suddenly there were daggers spinning toward her.

Chloe hissed and threw herself up into the air and backward.

Her claws extended and she grasped the back of a seat, knowing it would be there. Her legs came down and her foot claws came out, grabbing a seat in the next row. Suddenly she was terrified and powerful, hunted but in control.

She knelt on the narrow seat back, barely using her claw tips to balance.

"Ah, the animal comes out. This makes it easier," Alexander said, grinning. He threw a screaming silver dagger at her. He, too, was as he should be: the hunter.

Chloe turned and sprang from seat back to seat back, down to the front of the theater.

Keep it under control, she told herself. But it felt *so good* to be moving.

"Your sister was hard to kill," the Rogue taunted, running down the aisle to keep up with her.

My sister.

By the time Chloe found out she even had one, the girl was already dead. Thanks to Sergei. And the Rogue.

Rage exploded in her heart, burning her limbs. She took a last wild leap from the first row to the proscenium, twisting in the air so she landed facing the Rogue. Now she had higher ground: a distinct advantage.

"One last question," she growled. "Was it *you* following me all this time?"

"Unless there was someone else, yes," he said, jumping from the floor to the first row of seats. He ran along their backs as nimbly as a Mai. "But you're almost always surrounded by humans. We had to get you alone."

The Rogue launched himself forward, vaulting up onto the stage and landing neatly in a crouch.

Chloe threw herself at him before he was completely down, growling. It took all of her effort to resist instinct, which told her to just get him in the chest or the stomach, disemboweling him the way a cat would. But she could see that under his neoprene he had Kevlar armor rippling over his arms and chest.

She reached out with her claws, aiming for his throat, right above his matte black armor, his only exposed and vulnerable place.

The Rogue brought his arms together and up, holding a dagger diagonally down against his wrist to protect his throat. Her left claws clanged against metal, sending shivers up her arm like a nail bent backward. But her right claws got something; as she pushed herself off him there was blood, but she couldn't tell if it was on his hand or ear. The Rogue didn't scream; he just sucked in a choking lungful of air.

She flipped backward twice and landed fifteen feet away. Her hands came up, protecting her own throat, and she waited for him to react. If she turned her back and tried to run, even for a second, Chloe knew she'd have a dagger between her vertebrae.

This theater could easily become her mausoleum.

And she would wake up with him leaning over her, waiting, and he would take his little silver dagger and drag it across her throat. Seven times. Until she didn't wake up again.

Chloe panicked for a moment, filled with memories that weren't hers. A girl, running through the dark. A city at night. An alley. The dream she had—a tattoo on an arm. *Sodalitas Gladii Decimi. Her sister.*

The Rogue stood up, a little shakily, but he already had a shuriken in the hand that didn't have the dagger.

She had lost her concentration.

"FREEZE!"

Both of them turned.

The doors of the theater crashed open and a policeman stood there, his .45 drawn and aimed. It was hard to tell which one of them it was aimed *at*. It didn't matter; another appeared by his side and also clicked her safety off. A third came forward, saw the body, and ran forward to kneel by him.

"Both of you. PUT YOUR WEAPONS DOWN," the first policeman shouted.

For a split second Chloe and the Rogue shared a moment, looking at each other. Then at the same time—without a signal—they both began running in opposite directions. Chloe made for the emergency exit on the right side of the screen.

"I SAID FREEZE!" the policeman bellowed again.

She leapt forward off the stage, putting all of her strength into her arms and crouching into a cannonball. She crashed into the door, forcing it open as the first shot went off. It was *loud.* Louder than she could have believed from TV.

Chloe barreled through the door and rolled onto the pavement outside, just ducking and pulling her legs in before it swung hard shut behind her. Her knuckles were bloody and raw from protecting the top of her head.

She took off, running and leaping and jumping from hydrant to awning to fire escape to roof, grabbing and swinging until she was back on the skyline, where she could travel quickly and safely, where she belonged.

Fourteen

What now?

Chloe kept running but forced herself to *think*—something her cat instincts didn't like.

She had spent the last several weeks at home, recovering from a previous attempt on her life, integrating the relatively sudden manifestation of her new abilities, two death-resurrections, and the Order of the Tenth Blade, the Mai, and their relationship for the past thousand years into her normal teenage life.

But what *hadn't* she done?

"Prepare, make a safe room, dig out a Cat Cave," Chloe answered to the night air as she leapt across the gaps between buildings, ignoring the hundred-foot drops below. "Actually train myself in fighting. Come up with some sort of defensive strategy. Initiate an emergency or panic routine for me, Amy, and Paul to follow. And Kim. And Alyec. COME UP WITH A PLAN."

She cursed herself for not having done it sooner. *Complete denial mode does not save lives,* Chloe thought.

"A little late, Chlo," she muttered.

At least the Rogue probably wasn't following her. As strong and skilled as he was, Alexander was still human and couldn't make the sort of jumps or move at the pace she could. For a moment Chloe allowed herself to picture him in a Rogue-mobile, with an evil grinning face on the front like a blond Joker. Even if he did have a car, he was probably driving it as fast as possible away from the police without any regard for her.

"Thank God for the police," Chloe muttered, for once without irony. How did they know what was going on? How did they know that anyone was there?

She made for the tallest point on the local horizon before her, a large satellite dish that was screwed solidly but inexpertly to the top of a chimney. If anyone was coming after her—the police or the Rogue or whomever—she would see them coming.

Once carefully balanced on top, one claw wrapped around the rim of the dish, she pulled out the one weapon she had available to her.

Her cell phone.

First she dialed Firebird.

"'Allo, Firebird LLC," the receptionist's voice came over. *Someone should really tell her to cut the Russian accent on outside calls,* Chloe thought. She *knew* Alexandra could speak almost perfect English; at this point anything else was an affectation.

"It's Chloe. Get me Olga."

"She's out at the moment—can I take a message?"

"No. Get me Igor."

"Honored One, he is in a meeting," she responded deferentially but promptly.

"Get him out," Chloe said, rolling her eyes at the strange incongruity of the other woman's words. "It's *very* important."

"Yes, Honored One," Alexandra said, putting her on hold. Chloe was still amazed; the other girl obviously hadn't liked her from the beginning, and now she did whatever Chloe asked without hesitation and only a little sarcasm.

After a surprisingly short wait, Igor got on.

"Hello?" He sounded a little irritated and snappish. *Not so much into the whole spiritual leader thing.* Which was going to make what she had to say next that much worse.

"Igor, Sergei's dead."

There was a pause, as if he was wondering if he had heard right. Igor's English wasn't perfect, so that was understandable. "What are you talking about?" he finally said.

"The Rogue just killed Sergei. I was with him at the theater you guys are looking at." Later she would burden him with the details about how she was there so that Sergei could have her *killed;* for now she just wanted the news out.

"Wait, wait. The Rogue is still alive? I thought you killed him."

"No, in fact, I tried to *save*—oh, never mind." Chloe sighed. Someday she would straighten that story out, too. "Apparently he did *not* die falling from the Golden Gate Bridge. Somehow he lived. And he just killed Sergei at the theater."

"What theater?" Igor demanded, his voice rising.

"The theater you guys were thinking about buying and tearing down for apartments or something or other," Chloe said, exasperated he had chosen to fix on that particular point.

"We weren't about to buy any theater. . . . I don't know what you're talking about."

Chloe sat back on the rim of the dish, stunned. It was bad enough that Sergei had been trying to kill her, but the lengths he had gone to plan it . . . Having keys to a property that no one at Firebird knew about just to have a convenient place for Chloe to be killed. Having Olga look for Chloe's dad to give her a reason to meet them there. Was there anything Sergei didn't lie about—or anyone in the Pride he didn't lie to?

"Where is this theater?" Igor prodded. "I'll get there right away—"

"No," Chloe cut him off. "The place is crawling with police. They showed up right after the Rogue and I began going at it. Stay away—tell *everyone* to stay away, even the kizekh. We can't risk the exposure."

She couldn't believe she was talking like this.

"Are you sure he's dead?" Igor said in almost a whisper.

"I'm pretty sure, Igor," she said as gently as she could. "If there's any chance he's alive, they'll bring him to a hospital. But he looked pretty gone. I'm sorry."

There was a long pause.

"Did you kill the Rogue?" Igor finally asked with a deadly calm to his voice.

"What? No," Chloe said, knowing it was a mistake as the words came out of her mouth. "In front of all those police?"

"Did you pursue him at all?"

"No, Igor, I fled the scene. Did I *mention* the cops? With the guns?" She tried to sound equally calm and directed, not cowardly, like he probably thought she was. "Listen, I'll explain it all to you later, okay? There is a *lot* to explain. I'll come over tonight. But I have to go now." She hung up. *Why couldn't it have been Olga?* She was terrified, adrenalized, and now she felt like cowardly shit just because of Mr. Sergei's ultratestosterone Padawan.

Who was out there who would *sympathize* with her? Not accuse or question?

As she dialed, a police car sped by a hundred feet below her, its siren howling. Chloe turned to watch, but it didn't stop.

"Chloe!" Amy chirped on the other end. "What's up?"

"Remember Sergei? The old guy who was trading insults with the other old guy at the Presidio . . . ?"

"The leader of your Pride, yeah," her friend answered. Sounding smug that she knew all that.

"He's dead. Killed by that assassin who tried to kill me on the bridge."

"Oh my God!"

"But he was actually trying to have *me* killed by the Rogue; it was kind of a setup—"

"Holy shit," Amy interrupted. "What are you going to do?"

"I think . . ." Chloe thought about it. She had no desire to go over to Firebird immediately; it was probably a mess. And in the interest of full disclosure—since she was probably going to see it on the news anyway—it was probably best to come clean to her mother. "I think I'm actually going to go home. If anything weird is going to happen, I want to be able to protect her."

"Good thinking. Paul and I will go over, too. We might as well be all together since everyone already knows about us."

"I—okay, yeah, good idea."

"Absolutely. See you in a little while."

And now the last call. It was even set for speed dial.

"Hello?"

"Alyec." She took a deep breath. "Sergei's dead. The Rogue killed him."

"Oh my God! Are you okay?"

"I'm fine. I'm going home to make sure Mom's okay and everything. Don't know *what's* going to happen next."

"Do you need me? I'm kind of in the middle of band practice—but I'll drop everything and come if you want. . . ."

"No." Chloe smiled and shook her head, forgetting he couldn't see it. "I'm fine. Call me when you're out."

"Okay. Be safe, Chloe."

"I will."

Chloe clicked her phone off and shoved it back in her pocket. When she first was hunted by the Rogue and had developed her powers, she always took circuitous routes home to confuse anyone who might be following her. Since her mom's kidnapping it was obvious that *everyone* knew where she lived—now it was just important that she get there first. She took one last long look around, enjoying the view and the moment's respite from the horrors of what was to come next.

Then she leapt down to the rooftop and hurried home through alleys and back ways, invisible to everyone—including the police.

When she heard her mom jingling her keys at the door, she opened it but forgot to retract her claws and Anna started at the sight. Chloe had spent the hour before her mom got home from work patrolling the house, making sure the windows and doors were locked, and listening for the sounds of an intruder. Amy sat in front of the TV, flipping between *CNN Headline News* and local channels (and reruns of *Invader Zim*). Paul wasn't there yet.

"Not dipping into the catnip, are you?" Anna King asked a little nervously as she came in and put her attaché case on the counter.

"Not exactly," Chloe said with a wry smile.

"Hey—it's on again!" Amy called from the couch.

Mother and daughter moved farther into the living room. A grim-faced young newsman talked while the words *Local Businessman Murdered* lit up the corner of the screen in red, yellow, and blue.

"Local real estate magnate Sergei Shaddar was found dead today in an abandoned theater. Connie Brammeier in Inner Sunset has the story."

The camera switched to a female reporter, younger and serious, on the scene. Things were going on behind her, but it was hard to tell what exactly. There were policemen, a tired-looking detective who frowned over her clipboard, and flashes going off.

"Earlier today police were alerted by a local about suspicious activity in the condemned building. Inside they found the body of Sergei Shaddar, owner of Firebird Properties LLC, gruesomely—and possibly ritually—covered in stab wounds."

"Covered? There was only one," Chloe said before she stopped herself.

". . . his throat also cut. Whether this was some sort of gang-related activity or a random attack remains unknown. Shaddar was a reclusive but popular businessman who donated ten thousand dollars every Christmas to local charities."

That's news to me, Chloe thought. Like inverse variables and people who liked Avril Lavigne, it was hard to wrap her mind around someone who was so absolutely evil—*and* gave to the poor.

"Investigators say there is no trace of the two suspects who fled the scene, but police are looking into it. Anyone with information on this crime is encouraged to call the number at the bottom of the screen. All tips are kept anonymous. Bob?"

"Why do I get the feeling that one of the 'suspects' is *you,* Chloe?" her mom asked in what was dangerously close to a growl. Amy turned down the volume.

Chloe took a deep breath. "Sergei told me to meet him at that theater because he had information on Dad." Her mom's eyes widened. "He was setting me up to be killed by the Rogue, who was also there waiting for me."

"I thought that person—the Rogue—fell from the bridge," her mother said slowly.

"Two percent of suicides survive the fall every year," Amy said, not tearing her eyes from the television.

"Anyway, he's still alive," Chloe continued as her mom frowned. "He and Sergei were working together to kill any potential 'Chosen Ones'—for different reasons, obviously. They're the ones who killed my biological sister a few months ago. But the Rogue turned on Sergei and killed him before attacking me—just another Mai he wanted dead."

Anna King looked at her daughter for a long moment, unblinking, just like Kim. Her eyes were much harder and flintier than the cat girl's, and her blond hair wasn't as wispy as she usually kept it. When she finally spoke, it was as calmly as Igor.

"That's it. We're moving."

Chloe had to replay what she said several times before accepting it.

"What?"

"We're moving. San Francisco is way too dangerous. It's ridiculous." Anna King took her glasses off and turned away, getting a notepad. "I shouldn't have any trouble finding a job in Seattle or New York. . . ."

"Mom, what are you talking about?" Chloe followed her around. Amy sort of wilted back onto the couch, just peeping over the top.

"In the last few months, there have been *two* attempts on your life." Her mother ticked things off on her fingers. "*I've* been held hostage, *you've* been basically held hostage, I have personally witnessed a gang war, no matter what you want to call it."

"We can't just run away—the Mai have looked for me for so long—they won't just give up. And the Rogue will, too!" Chloe protested.

"Then we'll go into hiding. I'll tell the authorities about what happened to me and we'll go into a federal protection something or other. Start over. I don't care."

"I can't just *leave* everyone!" Chloe wailed, wishing she sounded less teenage-y.

"And *I* can't just let you die!" her mother shouted back. Her eyes blazed; her jaw was set with frustration.

Suddenly Chloe understood. Her mom felt helpless that she couldn't protect her daughter. She felt ignorant and left out; her daughter's life was suddenly flooded with ancient cults and mythological races and Anna was angry because she had no control. And that was one thing she treasured more than almost anything else.

Of course, the whole situation really *was* out of control: Sergei was dead, the Rogue was still on the loose, Brian was probably still on the Order's hit list, the Mai were leaderless and lost, and, Chloe slowly realized, there was only one person who could fix it.

She squared her shoulders and kept her voice calm. "Mom, I know this is all upsetting, but running away really won't fix anything. The Mai can track me like bloodhounds. And . . . I *can't* leave them. I'm their only leader now." When her mom opened her mouth, Chloe gently cut her off. "*You* saw me die and rise from the dead. You see my claws. This isn't just a high-school varsity club or something—this is serious. And I'm the only one who can stop this cycle of violence," Chloe found herself saying. *Wow, do I really believe that?* When she thought about it, she realized it *wasn't* a "belief"; it was a truth. She *had* to be the one who stopped it. Or else it would keep on going. Forever.

Or until everyone involved was dead.

"And *I* can't let you keep on being involved," her mother said shakily. But Chloe could hear her resolve cracking.

"Neither you *nor* I have that choice," Chloe said. "If I don't go to them, they'll come to us. And I swore you would never get hurt again."

"Why can't I swear that about my own daughter?" Anna whispered, putting her fingers to her temple. She wasn't crying, not quite, but it was obvious she was holding it back.

Then someone knocked on the door, causing everyone to jump.

"Hey," Paul yelled cheerily through the glass, holding up a bag of Krispy Kremes. Then he saw the looks on everyone's faces. "Did I come at a bad time?"

Her mom insisted on driving if she couldn't forbid or direct. Paul and Amy sat in the backseat, stuffing themselves with doughnuts to get through the tension.

Almost like old times, Chloe thought wistfully. Something about being in the passenger seat made her feel like she was ten again. Her mother's jaw was still clenched, teeth gritted; even her earrings swung determinedly from her ears.

Chloe sighed, tracing the little bits of rain that built up on the window before marching their way down to the side and bottom, held up against the glass by wind. Someone once said something about a leader being only as good as the friends and advisers she surrounded herself with. *Maybe I should give Paul and Amy a little more credit.*

When they arrived at Masa—the restaurant was as neutral a meeting ground as any—they were led discreetly to the back, where Olga, Igor, and Kim were already waiting. Her mother's eyes bulged when they all said, "Welcome home, Honored One," and bowed. Chloe gave her mom a weak grin and shrugged.

It was a rectangular table and Chloe immediately made for one of the long sides, next to Olga, but her mother nudged her and shook her head the slightest bit, indicating the head of the table with her eyes.

"If you really want to stop the violence and lead your people, you have to *lead* them," she murmured. "*Take* control, Chloe. No one's going to take it for you."

Chloe nodded, seeing something in Anna King's eyes that she'd never really paid attention to before. Something that involved a high-powered job and politics. Something about being a woman and a partner at a major firm. *I'll have to ask her about that someday,* Chloe thought, slipping into the chair, sinking into its soft leather. She tried to concentrate on the impression the ass of the previous person had made on the seat to avoid the nervous feeling in her stomach.

Igor and Olga were obviously surprised and uncomfortable with the unscheduled presence of the humans.

"Igor, Olga, this is my mom, Anna King." Chloe indicated with her hand. Olga got over whatever shock she felt and shook hands warmly.

"It is so nice to meet you," she said in her thick accent—which got noticeably thicker whenever she was stressed.

"Hello," Igor said curtly.

"My friends, Paul and Amy."

The two Mai nodded at the two human teenagers; neither Olga nor Igor had been at the fight at the Presidio. *They were busy getting actual work done,* she thought with a mental snort. Not playing power games like the two old men who ruled both sides.

"This is Olga and Igor, the Mai's top two, uh, officials," Chloe said.

"Nice to meet you," her mom said, a little coldly.

"Paul, Amy." Olga nodded in their direction. "Mrs. King."

Kim just gave a little wave—somehow completely adorable with her cat paws.

"You *know* these people?" Igor asked her, astounded.

"They're my friends," Kim said nonchalantly

"I'm sorry if I compromised security," Chloe said, indicating that the other Mai should sit down, too, as well as her mom. All three did, looking at each other a little distrustfully. "I . . . wasn't sure what was going to happen next and I wanted to keep them safe."

"Of course," Olga said promptly. "They helped save you, yes? They are certainly welcome with us."

Igor didn't say anything.

"Before we go any further with anything . . ." Chloe took a deep breath. "You should know that Sergei was trying to have me killed when this happened."

Kim's eyes widened until they looked like they were going to pop out of their sockets. Olga slowly shook her head.

"That's ridiculous," Igor said.

"Unfortunately, it's not." She told them the whole story, as accurately and in as much detail as she could remember it. Especially Sergei's exact words.

"So basically Sergei and the Rogue had been working together to find and kill all other possible Chosen Ones, including *my sister.*"

"There's no reason," Igor scoffed.

"He wanted to keep power, and he was afraid of it being taken away."

"But you are the One," Olga said helplessly. "Why would he do that?"

"I *just* told you," Chloe said, trying not to lose patience. Her mom gave the slightest shake of her head: *Calm down, Chloe.*

"I don't believe it," Igor said again, taking a gulp of his coffee.

"Okay, believe it or don't; the fact is that he's *dead*

and the police are making an investigation. What do we do now?"

Everyone around the table was quiet. Olga delicately sipped tea the waiter had brought. "We'll talk about it at the meeting with you and all of the Pride tomorrow night," she said.

"I'll teach you the main opening prayer phrase; I think that will be enough for now," Kim volunteered.

"*Prayer . . . ?*" Chloe's mom turned to glare at the cat girl. Kim's ears flattened and she shrank under the older woman's look.

"More of an—an invocation," she stuttered, "a traditional opening to a speech."

Chloe tried not to smile.

"Let me be entirely clear on one thing: I don't entirely approve of all this," Anna King said firmly, "though I respect the needs and beliefs of Chloe's native people. But if *anything* happens to Chloe, just remember: unlike you and the Order, I have nothing against guns."

Igor started to roll his eyes, but Olga kicked him under the table. Chloe imagined her mom posed with an automatic, screaming and waving the weapon back and forth, firing round after round at unseen enemies. In Chloe's vision she still had her reading glasses on and her swinging silver earrings.

"What do we tell everyone right now? About why you're not there with them?" Igor demanded.

"You tell them the truth." *Dipshit,* Chloe almost

added. "That it's really dangerous right now, that the Rogue is hot on my tail—that I'll see all of them tomorrow back at the Cat Cave."

"What?" Olga asked, startled.

Whoops. It's only funny to me, Chloe realized. "Uh—Firebird." But Paul and Amy were smiling. "You *also* tell them that there is to be *no retaliation*. Not from individuals, not from the kizekh."

"But loyal Mai will insist," Igor sputtered. "If I myself had the skills . . ."

"You—tell—them—there—will—be *no retaliation*," Chloe said again slowly. "No one is to do anything until after the big speechifying tomorrow night. Everyone's eager for blood—and the Tenth Blade will be prepared and waiting once they see the news. They'll be *expecting* an attack." She hoped this sounded reasonable.

"She's right," Olga said. Chloe was still stunned at the older woman's absolute faith in her as the Chosen One. She had been just as loyal to Sergei as Igor but had no problem accepting what the new, teen spiritual leader of the Mai said, no matter how far-fetched.

And it's a good thing, too, considering the dagger eyes Igor's giving me. . . .

"I believe we have a few hours lull before the storm," Kim added. "It would be a good time to take stock and make plans."

"Isn't the investigation of Sergei going to lead the police back to you guys?" Paul asked. "I mean, they're

going to look at Firebird and all of his business associ-
ates and disgruntled employees. . . ."

"That's right," Chloe's mom said. "Do you guys
even *have* a plan for that kind of investigation?"

Igor and Olga looked at each other, then at Chloe.

Apparently *not*.

Fifteen

The next morning Chloe realized it was a Tuesday. But instead of going to school, she stayed in bed for a while and decided that with everything that was going on around her, one more day wouldn't be the end of the world. She couldn't deal with anything else right now. No after school makeups, no seeing anyone, no nothing. Nothing until seven o'clock that night, when she had to address the tiny tribe of homeless, leaderless Mai, over a hundred people she didn't know, slit-eyed faces upturned to her, looking for hope.

Chloe decided to treat it like an oral report and not worry about it until later. She stretched and sat up, letting her claws emerge for just a moment from the tips of her fingers and toes. Her pajamas were an old pair of boxers and a giant Tide T-shirt her mom had gotten free at Target or something. Big. Orange. Ugly.

Alyec liked her in frumpy, oversized nightclothes, she remembered a little sadly.

Chloe shook her head. She had made peace with him last week along with her homework. She had made peace with Marisol. *And Sergei is, uh, at peace.* Now she needed a day of peace and quiet for herself, before the shit started going down again that evening.

I need to go on a bike ride.

She showered off the night ick and pulled on clean jeans, a T-shirt, and a Patagonia fuzzy she rarely wore to school for fear of Amy accusing her of being crunchy. Her mom was downstairs at the table, sipping coffee and going over bills.

"I'm going to go for a ride," Chloe said, jerking her thumb in the direction of the mini-garage that held almost too much storage crap to fit the car anymore.

"Wear your helmet," her mother said automatically. Then she looked up at her daughter. "Wait? Are you sure you should? What about the police . . . and the Rogue?"

"Screw 'em," Chloe said with a fierce grin. Then she softened at the look on her mom's face. "I doubt the police would even recognize me with a helmet. As for the Rogue—I promise I'll stay in public places. He won't do anything if there are innocent people—humans—around. I really need to clear my head for a while."

"Me too," Anna King said distantly. "This is . . . really . . . unusual stuff for me to deal with, you know?"

"You totally didn't know what you were getting into

when you adopted me, huh?" She said it with a smile, but inside Chloe felt really guilty about it.

"I realized what I was getting into when you were two and you pulled the bookshelf down on top of you. And *then* began chewing on all of my favorite Tony Hillermans," her mom said archly. "I've been reading about other parents with children who want to reconnect with their . . . original *ethnicity*. But none of the case histories in it deal with the supernatural."

That was a strange word. Chloe had never actually thought about it in reference to herself. Well, she tried not to think about the whole dying-and-coming-back-to-life thing in general. It was too weird. Was Sergei in that place of shadows now? Did he exist with the other lion shadows who prowled the darkness in that eternity? Or was there a Mai hell reserved for people like him?

"The good news is, if I get into an accident, I have seven lives left," Chloe said with a grin.

"Don't even joke," her mother growled.

In some ways, Mom's a better embodiment of the Twin Goddesses than Kim, Chloe thought as she pedaled to the park. Like when she made that speech about protecting or avenging her daughter if something happened to her—protective like Bastet, warlike like Sekhmet. Kim was deeply spiritual but didn't really exhibit the qualities of either. If there was something like one of the Muses in the Mai pantheon, that would surely be Kim.

The air was crisp, perfect biking weather, the sun warm on her back. Amy used to make fun of Chloe's helmet when they were growing up—she always ditched hers as soon as they were out of sight of home. But Chloe thought it made her look like a real biker, like a racer or maybe a messenger girl.

People smiled at her as she took a path into Golden Gate Park; other cyclists said "Good morning" or "Great day for a ride." Chloe was both anonymous and recognized, greeted and then forgotten like all of the other people enjoying the nice day outside. A little kid on a pink bike with training wheels tried to race her a few feet and Chloe pretended to pedal furiously until the mom called her daughter back.

It was nice feeling her legs pump, the strange hunch as she leaned over the handlebars. But there was none of the familiar burn in her legs that she normally got, which was kind of ironic, really. The whole reason she'd wanted the Merida was because it had an electric pedal-assist motor and would require little effort on her part to take it up hills. With her Mai strength and endurance it wasn't an issue anymore. *I'll bet I could totally do triathlons now.* Except for maybe the swimming part—she wasn't sure how good cats were at swimming or how much their natural aversion would affect her performance.

She biked past the people who played ultimate early every morning and watched a tall, brown-haired guy leap for a high-thrown Frisbee. Farther on there was some typical San Francisco–style political stuff going on: a shortish blond guy who didn't look much older than she was standing at a table and handing out leaflets on the benefits of libertarianism. Chloe wasn't quite sure what that was, but judging from the jeers of some surrounding grunge types, it probably wasn't leftist.

She swung her bike hard to the north, exiting the park scant minutes later. The destination that had been troubling her in the back of her mind finally surfaced and made itself known: the Golden Gate Bridge.

The place where she had first fought the Rogue and thought he had died. The symbolic gap between her old life and the life of the Mai, holed up in their little mansion across the water in Sausalito. She and Amy and Paul—back when they were just a little younger, back when they were all still "just friends"—used to walk across it and dream of new worlds on the other side. After September 11 legions of National Guard were stationed around it, keeping it safe while making the locals uneasy.

What had once been one of her favorite places in the world had become a source of trepidation for her, of turmoil and serious stomach upset.

It's time to take it back. To reclaim it.

Chloe switched the bike to high gear and pumped as hard as she could, her legs outworking the motor. Trying not to think, she pushed herself forward and closed her eyes.

When she opened them, she was on the bridge.

It was a glorious day: the orange girders shining in defiance against the soft blue sky and cotton candy clouds, a color completely out of place in nature. The bay sparkled blindingly below, a dark blue on which powder white sailboats rode carelessly by. The hills in front of her were different glowing shades of green and dark green, like a watercolor poster in a tourist shop.

Chloe felt like shouting or singing. Since she couldn't really do the latter, she let out a, "WHOOOPPPEEE!" that scared several walkers.

Chloe was filled with a happiness in movement she hadn't felt in a long time. No hunting, no being hunted, no one around she knew to upset this; just the speed, the wind in her ears, her legs moving, the glorious view.

The prayer is the movement.

Chloe remembered something vaguely about Hopi snake dancers who prayed for rain with rattlesnakes in their mouths. The prayer *was* the dance, not a separate recitation or song or spoken verse. That was what she felt like now: all glory and joy in just being alive.

Thank you, Whoever.

The bridge was far too short in retrospect; as she passed over the other limit, Chloe wondered how it had seemed so endless those times she had driven back and forth, once with Brian nearly dying in the backseat.

She had no desire to return home yet, so she crossed over and made her way up the Marin Headlands, waiting to become tired as the hills took their toll on her legs.

It never happened.

As though she were spiraling to the tip of a giant soft-serve ice cream cone, Chloe coasted around the side of the hill and was confronted with another glorious view: the bridge from above, San Francisco in the distance, water and spray in between. There was only a small parking space and a thin coating of grass on the rocky promontory; most people came up, took a picture, and left. Those who stayed were respectful and quiet. Any noise from ecstatic children leaping at the top of the world was whipped away by the ocean wind.

Chloe carefully leaned her bike up against a boulder and climbed on top of it, hugging her knees to her chest and sucking in the view.

I wish I could feel this way forever.

Chloe wished there was some way to store this entire moment, not just the visual image, but smells and feelings and all. Like in a stone or something that she could keep in her jewelry box and take out when she needed to relive the moment.

Chloe leaned back and lay on her back, looking up at the sky. In the sun and the wind and silence the cogs in her mind slowly began to fall back into place; the monkey wrenches and other acts of mental sabotage from the last few months slowly disappeared. The background chatter in her brain quieted. She just *was*.

And there, hidden by the mental graffiti, were the

answers that had always been there. It wasn't a great revelation, a message from the Twin Goddesses or her mom or the beyond; it was just Chloe. Speaking clearly to herself.

She sat up and pulled out her phone, regretful that the moment was over but resolved.

She called information so that her phone number wouldn't show up on caller ID and asked for Whitney Rezza when she was patched through, telling the receptionist that it was Chloe King.

"Why, here's a call I never expected," Whitney said with his usual light sneer, like someone at a yacht club.

"Mr. Rezza, Alexander Smith killed Sergei yesterday."

"Really? Now, *that's* kind of unexpected. Good for him."

Chloe kept her inner calm, refusing to snap or get sarcastic. "Actually, the two were working together. To kill all descendants of the previous *true* Pride Leader. Like my sister. And me."

"I don't believe that for a moment," the older man said promptly.

Chloe wondered briefly if anyone on *either* side had ever seen a spy movie. Of any sort. It was like the idea that two enemies working together for a common goal was preposterous.

"Well, they were. I know: I was there when the Rogue killed him. They both talked about it. But look, that's not really why I called."

"Oh?"

"As the new Pride Leader—the *Chosen One*—I am offering a truce." She took a deep breath. She wasn't overstepping her authority; she *was* the new leader. People like Igor would have to just toe the line.

Right?

"We'll let the death of Sergei be the last violence between us. On my word," Chloe said with resolve.

"Hmmm . . . a fascinating idea . . ."

Chloe held her breath.

". . . but no, sorry, not that interested. This is the first time in years our Order has had a cause worth coming together for; why settle for a truce when we can proceed to wipe out the rest of you? I really should thank you, you know. . . . The little showdown at the Presidio you arranged really did wonders for our morale and purpose."

What did that mean? *There is power in war, that's what that means,* Chloe realized grimly. Their last major strategic maneuver against the Mai was when Whitney lost his wife to a random gang member who was unconnected with anyone. . . . Since then, the Order had been little more than a bunch of violent, slightly overglorified Masons, with secret rules and rituals but not much in the way of actual targeted attacks.

"I mean, good luck as the new leader and all—but really, they're going to be a bit like chickens with their heads cut off for a while, aren't they?"

He sounded so smug. Chloe needed one last thing, one card that would leave him disturbed. Give him something to think about.

"Thank you. By the way, Whitney, how's your son?" And with that, she hung up.

Secrecy. That was the problem on both sides. Secrecy and ritual. If it had been *her,* if *she* had been leader of the Mai years ago when they first came to America, at the first sign of attack from the Order she would have immediately had the top lawyer on racial crimes/crimes of hate on their ass. Blown their cult public. Paul had once shown her the list "Top 10 Things Not to Do as an Evil Overlord" on the Web, and in the top ten was that when the gang of heroes approaches, you do *not* unleash the hounds of hell upon them; you call the local police and have them arrested for trespassing.

I'm telling, Chloe decided, in as whiny and childish a mental voice as she could manage. She called information again and had herself redirected to the tip line that was on the news before.

"Hi? I have some, uh, information on the guy who was murdered in the movie theater yesterday?"

"Can you come down to the station so we can take a full report?" the person at the other end asked in a brusque and businesslike fashion.

"I'd, uh, rather not. I was, uh, buying some . . . *stuff* from a . . . *friend* inside—I saw the whole thing, but I don't want to get involved."

"All right," the woman grumbled, "tell me what you saw."

Chloe told her the entire story, skirting around her own presence as a member of the scene and focusing on the Rogue and Sergei. She described both perfectly—which finally got the other person's attention; it was obvious that Chloe wasn't just repeating what she saw on the news because she described the shuriken that went flying into Sergei's throat. She told them everything she could remember about the Rogue, from his dumb ponytail to the slashes on his arm, and added vague rumors from "on the street" about an insane guy with knives and a penchant for Hong Kong–style fighting. The policewoman thanked her and hung up.

"There," Chloe said, picking up her bike. "I *told*. Deal with *that*, Whitney Rezza."

Abiding by her new policy of no more secrets, Chloe decided to drive to the Firebird mansion that night without bothering to try and hide her tracks. It was ridiculous, anyway; Whitney knew who Sergei was, and *everyone* knew that Sergei ran Firebird. *And for that matter, the same probably holds true for the Tenth Blade.* All of Whitney's friends must have known he belonged to some private club—it wouldn't take a genius to follow him there one day.

Strangely, her mom didn't have a problem with her

borrowing the car. Technically speaking, even though Chloe only had a learner's permit, Anna King decided that her daughter was safer with access to wheels than just showing up in a taxi.

"You call me every half hour," her mother insisted. "If you miss one and I mean *one* phone call, I'm calling the police. You understand?"

"Yes, Mom." She didn't even say it sarcastically. Frankly, Chloe was amazed that her mom was letting her go so easily.

"And let's have a word . . . I know, 'David Bowie.' If you say that, then I'll call the police—okay? Those will be our safe words."

"Okay," Chloe agreed, wondering how she could work the rock star's name into casual conversation while her captors/tormentors were listening. "But I think I might need to stay there overnight. . . ."

"Then call me every three hours after 1 a.m., and I *mean* it, Chloe King. You may be their leader, but you're still my daughter, and you're still under eighteen."

"Yes, Mom," Chloe agreed dutifully. She had already planned on keeping the GPS phone on the whole time. So far, none of the Mai besides Kim and Alyec knew about it.

By the time Chloe arrived at Firebird, the sun had set—and the news on TV had changed.

"I think you'd better look at this, Chloe." Kim had

been waiting for Chloe in the driveway, perched on top of the ornate marble fountain that marked the center of the turnaround in front of the entrance. She looked worried, which panicked Chloe: her friend usually didn't react to *anything*.

No one was in the lobby; no one was in any of the offices. *Many* of the top people were in Sergei's office, their slit eyes wide and dismayed in the half-light, soaking up the rays of the giant TV he had behind a curtain.

There was another reporter outside the theater, talking, but the photos being flashed in the corner when he turned the story back over to the deskman weren't of Sergei—they were of people he had murdered.

Chloe focused on the TV and serious-looking reporter on-screen.

". . . now that the FBI is involved. Investigators report that Sergei Shaddar was a criminal mastermind involved in some Eastern Bloc terrorist organizations. Information from Georgian officials suggest that many of the murders he carried out in his homeland were disguised under the cover of civil violence between the Georgians and the breakaway state Abkhazia."

Chloe looked at Kim. "Keep watching," the other girl whispered. "It gets crazier."

"Shaddar was also involved in a number of other murders in the United States, possibly including the murder of a girl whose wounds and method of murder perfectly match those of Mr. Shaddar."

A photo of the girl who had been Chloe's sister was shown in the corner now.

Believe me yet, jerky? Chloe wanted to mutter to Igor, but that wouldn't have been a very leaderlike thing to do.

Instead she sighed, shook her head, then raised her voice, flipping on the lights.

"Could everyone who isn't Olga, Igor, or Kim please leave the room?"

Everyone turned to face her, blinking against the bright light. A dozen pairs of eyes went back to nearly humanlike round pupils.

"And please ready the, uh, auditorium for the seven o'clock meeting. Could one of you make sure that there's a TV, with access to the news, or a giant projection screen, or something like that?"

Heads nodded: "Yes, Honored One." Chloe tried not to notice how relieved and grateful and hopeful the faces were as they passed and looked at her. Even the receptionist who had sneaked in behind them to watch the news bowed her head.

When they were all gone, Kim closed the door.

"Anyone want to say anything?" Chloe asked, looking back and forth between the three of them.

Olga took the opportunity to start crying. "I never knew!" She coughed. "I can't believe . . ."

Her eyes went slitty again and her claws came out as emotions overcame her; Chloe realized that of all the

202

Mai she knew even a little, not once had she seen the older woman transform at all.

"I can't believe it either," Igor said softly, but the blank look in his eyes said otherwise. "He was like a father to me. . . ."

"May I suggest a little perspective?" Kim asked in one of the coldest tones Chloe had ever heard her use. "In other orphan cases like Chloe's the human parents have 'randomly' disappeared or turned up dead, like with Chase. . . . You cannot tell me you didn't suspect *something*."

Neither of the other two said anything. Olga looked vaguely shamefaced, however.

"Don't ask, don't tell, huh? All right, the past is the past," Chloe said. She fought a surge of disgust and anger as she thought of her own mom and the traces of Mai presence that Kim had found around her house. "I am declaring an official moratorium and amnesty right now. In the future, there will be *no more murders*. And if someone suspects something, it gets dealt with *normally* through the police—not covered up, okay? Listen." Chloe looked at her watch. "I have to call my mom in, like, five minutes, but before then I want to reveal some of my secret plans."

Plans that she had worried about and gone over in her head and had found nothing wrong with—but that she still doubted.

"Igor, until—well, until further notice, you're now

acting president of Firebird. Olga, consider yourself CEO." The Mai boy blinked a couple of times at this in a way that wasn't entirely human, shocked out of his snit by the sudden weight of responsibility. Chloe went on. "No matter *what* happens, real estate is not in my future, and human resources is not in my immediate future, as nice as the thought of finding more misplaced Mai may be. I really do plan on going to college. Oh, and let me reiterate one last time—" Chloe fixed her eyes on Igor's. "Sergei. And the Rogue. Were working. *Together.* Which revelation will also no doubt appear in the news sometime in the next few hours after the police release the information."

"How do you know that?" Igor asked, plainly mystified.

"Because *I* told them," Chloe answered smugly. It was true: not in a million years did either side expect the other to go to the police.

The call to her mom was fast, the walk to the auditorium faster. Finally events were catching up with her, the calmness of the afternoon replaced by nerves over what she had to do in the next hour. Public speaking was *not* one of Chloe's finer talents. It didn't help that Kim wore a traditional off-white linen robe and makeup that was sort of Egyptian, kohl black around her eyes and under her chin. She tried to get Chloe to wear a robe, too.

"It's not my thing," Chloe flatly refused. "Our people

should see what kind of a person I really am—not pretending to be."

Kim didn't argue.

The room was smaller than she expected; there really were only a hundred cat people, like a studio audience, ten by ten and packed. While it was a relief, it was also kind of sad: there were only three Prides in America, and this was one of them, and there were so few. . . . Chloe was the leader of a dying people, an endangered race.

Someone had set up the projection TV as she had asked, and all watched, horrified, the news about their old leader flicker across the screen through reporters' mouths and on a colorful banner at the bottom. When she thought they had seen enough, Chloe nodded at the guy in the back—*Mai A/V geek?*—and went out on the little stage, behind Kim.

Her friend, now completely in her role of priestess, held out her hands, closed her eyes, and began to sing. Like the night of the Hunt, when Chloe had first heard a traditional Mai chant, this was just as strange and wailing. It was impossible to predict where the melody would go; Kim changed tone and octave without warning. It sounded as sad and alien as Chloe felt her people looked right then.

Suddenly she *felt* them right then.

As the hymn continued and she looked out at the faces, Chloe could feel the collective emotions of the group. *Fear. Sadness. Expectation. We are so few! We have lost so many! And now this . . .*

Hope, as they looked at her.

Igor was trying to pay attention, but feelings of betrayal and pain were so strong that he wasn't really connected to the others.

She felt strange warmth, like everyone was where they should be: here they were, her Pride, together, waiting for her.

There was one off note, one small thing missing, like someone wasn't there.

After Kim finished, Chloe stepped up, no longer afraid or nervous. Here were her people. She was their leader. She cleared her throat.

"For those of you who haven't met me yet, I am Chloe King, Pride Leader and your Chosen One."

It sounded so stilted and strange, but everyone was listening raptly.

"Sergei Shaddar was *not* your true leader. Though he had good intentions, they were carried out with evil means. The man you thought you were following to some sort of happy-ever-after brought only violence and death. Even those closest to him had no idea of the extent of his activities." *Of course, the kizekh probably had a pretty good idea, since he must have used them to carry out some of his directives. . . .* But she would stick to her line of amnesty and forgiveness.

"When I met with him at the theater where he was

killed, the Rogue was already there, waiting for me."

There was no noise from the reserved Mai, but Chloe felt the collective shock of a hundred people.

"The two had been working together to kill *all* possible Chosen Ones, including my sister. I don't know if Sergei actually killed any himself, but he told the Rogue where she would be and where I would show up, and Alexander did the rest. Once he had me in his sights, Sergei was also no longer any use to him and the Rogue killed him as well."

"I cannot believe a Mai would kill another Mai! There are so few of us," a Mai wailed.

"There are bad people even among us, just as there are good people among the humans, like my mom. And Brian. And Paul and Amy."

Scanning the small crowd, she saw Alyec. Their eyes locked for a moment and he smiled—genuinely, without what had happened between them recently getting in the way. Supporting her. She smiled back without thinking.

"My mother, your previous Chosen One—it was her dream to unite all of the Eastern European Mai, those who had been scattered by war and exile and violence and our curse.

"As your *new* Pride Leader, I believe it is time now that we are all together to embrace our new land fully." There was a little hesitation at this—they were *not* all here yet, and where was she going with this? "Sergei was right about one more thing—you *shouldn't* have to live here like rats holed up. You should be free to pursue your own destinies and come together because you want to, not because you're forced to.

"You're in America now, in some ways no different from any other immigrants. From now on we abide by its laws. That means *no more* revenge and wars with the Tenth Blade. They break the law—they will be punished accordingly. As you might have seen from the news, they are hot in pursuit of the Rogue. And you know why? *Because I told them he was Sergei's murderer.*"

This time there was an audible gasp.

Kim was off to one side, Chloe suddenly noticed, talking with whoever it was running the TV.

"The police will track him down and arrest him. He will be punished for this and his other crimes. . . ."

"Chloe," Kim murmured, coming to her side, "forgive me for interrupting, but Ivan has told me there's something on the news we should see—he TiVo'ed the last few minutes. . . ."

"Put it on." Kim nodded to the back and the projection television came on again.

Somehow Chloe wasn't surprised to see a photo of her biological mother appear next to the CNN guy's face, as one of the dead counted by Sergei's hand.

". . . Anastasia Leon, member and leader of an obscure tribe of Eastern European nomads, originally from Turkey, had returned to her people's homeland.

208

Investigators are now turning up evidence that she was one of the first of Sergei Shaddar's political murders; the sources are unsure why. . . ."

Anastasia Leon. That was her mother's name. And there she was. A photo similar to the one that Chloe had held in her hand just a couple of weeks ago, of a woman with waist-length black hair and a wide, untamed smile, furrowed brow and determined eyes.

She gestured for the sound to be turned back down.

The Mai looked stunned; some were weeping, some growling. Chloe felt a mix of pity and bewilderment that *none* of them had seen this coming.

"See? This is *exactly* what I'm talking about. Secrecy and survival has forced you to follow a man who *murdered* your Pride Leader. This causeless violence between us and the Tenth Blade ends *now*. All it does is breed more violence and plays for power among ourselves—look what Sergei did to my sister, and look what Brian's people did to *him*.

"I am your new Chosen One, and I will lead you to safety and prosperity—but only through peace."

There was a pause. Were they going to clap? Drum her out? What happened next? Chloe desperately tried to feel the strange empathy she had experienced before, but it had faded to a dull heartbeat.

Suddenly Alyec leapt to his feet and roared. The only time Chloe had ever heard anything like it was when she'd lost her cool with Keira—and scared the bejesus out of the other girl. It was a deep, frightening sound that seemed much too loud and deep for his human frame to produce. His eyes were slit and scary; his claws were out.

Valerie stood up next and joined him.

Soon everyone was standing and howling and roaring, a deafening clamor that should have frightened Chloe but didn't. For just a moment the link was back and she could feel their energy and power and love—the support of the Pride.

Kim didn't roar, choosing to give her a strangely human thumbs-up.

When Chloe retired to give her mom a quick call, letting her know how it went, she was exhausted. *Still not a public speaker,* she realized. Just able to do it when called for. Igor waited patiently close by for her to get off the phone.

"Honored One . . . ?" he asked politely.

"Yes, Igor?" Chloe asked as she set down the phone. Soon she would get back on the bandwagon of making them call her Chloe. It seemed too much to do right now, though.

"I wanted to say . . . I think you are right." It didn't look like he was forcing himself to say this; he seemed full of the stillness and peace that she herself had experienced that afternoon. "Maybe it's because I deal—dealt—with humans more than Sergei, but we should follow their laws. Especially if we stay. And even if we don't stay—nomads can't make asses of themselves everywhere they go. Otherwise we won't be welcomed back." There was the faintest smile on his lips.

"Thanks, Igor. That really means a lot to me." And that was it—it was over. All of the tension between them for the last few days, all of his irritation at her. But the sadness was still there, and Chloe knew that he would be thinking a lot about Sergei in the upcoming weeks, remembering the good things while sifting through them, looking for signs of the ruthless killer beneath. "I never knew my biological father," she added softly. "And my adopted dad skipped out when I was little. Sergei was the third father I lost—and in some ways, the one I was closest to."

Igor nodded, not trusting himself to speak.

"Hey," Chloe said, changing the subject and remembering the absence she had felt at the beginning of the speech. "Where's Dmitry, by the way?"

He was the bodyguard Sergei had assigned to her when she was feeling rebellious living with the Mai, the one who came to protect her when they went out to see *Star Wars*. Along with Ellen, another member of the kizekh—and, she was pretty sure, his lover.

She was expecting a quick answer, like, *Oh, he patrols and guards the upstairs while the Pride meets to keep them safe.*

But Igor's face, blank and confused, told another story.

This is one of those loose ends, Chloe realized tiredly. *One of those unexplained things that's gonna come back and bite me in the ass later.* She was getting so much wiser so quickly . . . and it didn't make her happier.

Sixteen

Eventually Chloe was able to quietly extract herself from the crowd and slip away to the hospital room. Brian was actually reading, beneath a single light floating alone in the darkness.

"Hey," she said, smiling.

"Hey." He put down his book and looked up at her eagerly. There was one thin bandage around his head now, mostly white and unstained. His hair was a little fluffier, like it had been cleaned, and his eyes were brighter, though they were still surrounded by bruises and cuts. But there was definitely something more *alive* about him, pink and healthy, and Chloe felt a little rush of pride that maybe, just maybe, she'd been the one to lift the age-old human-Mai curse.

The book, Chloe noticed as she came closer, was *Blood Meridian*. It looked like a Western.

"Not a lot of reading choices down here," he said, shrugging. "But this is pretty good."

"Are they treating you okay?" she asked, pulling up a metal stool.

"Are you *kidding?*" Brian snorted. "Whatever they think of me, they keep it to themselves. It's all 'Honored One' this and 'Chosen One' that and 'as she desires. . . .' Although the doctor, I think, really *is* good. And kind of funny, for a Mai."

"What's *that* supposed to mean?" Chloe demanded, taking his hand.

"As someone who has been forced to study them most of his life, I gotta tell you: most of your compatriots don't really have much of a sense of humor."

Chloe opened her mouth to disagree, then thought about it. He was right.

She shrugged. "We had a big powwow upstairs."

"I heard. Well, I didn't actually *hear,* but everyone was talking about it. Everything okay?"

Chloe sighed and told him about Sergei and the Rogue and her reporting it to the police and the subsequent follow-up investigations and how he appeared to have killed her entire biological family except for her dad, who no one knew or seemed to really care about. She had to stop once to call her mom, which Brian later teased her about, but he sat quietly, eyes twinkling, while she called.

"Well." She stretched, yawning. "That's about it."

"What now?"

"Now?" She extended her claws without thinking

214

and scratched at a particularly itchy spot on her head. She hoped it wasn't dandruff. Or whatever cats got. "Now I think I find my old bedroom, crawl into bed, and sleep until hell freezes over—or I have to call my mom again, in about three hours."

"Why don't you stay here?" Brian suggested quietly.

Chloe looked at him. He wasn't kidding. In fact, she had never seen him look at her more seriously. He reached out a hand and touched her lips—a hand that was connected to a really toned arm, peach-colored and muscled. He moved his fingers along her cheek and jaw to run his hand through her hair.

Then she eased off the stool and lowered the metal side of his hospital bed.

"It will be just like a sleepover," he said, grinning.

"No pillow fights for you," she murmured, pulling back the sheet and kissing his neck.

In the morning, Chloe woke up cramped and sleepy.

She had only missed one phone call to her mom— the 4 a.m. one—and Anna King had called her at exactly five minutes past. While it wasn't exactly convenient to answer, the consequences would have been far worse, so Chloe had forced herself to.

Brian made little murmuring noises as she carefully disengaged herself and slid off the side of the bed.

"C'm back soon," he mumbled, trying to open his eyes and failing. "Miss you."

Chloe leaned over and kissed him. Brian smiled but was soon snoring again.

How do I feel? Chloe asked herself, picking her jeans up off the floor and putting them on. They fit softly and nicely, like third-day jeans always did.

Do I feel different?

She made her way through the benches of hospital-y stuff, surprising Dr. Lovsky, who was carrying a breakfast tray for Brian.

"Oh, uh, morning, Honored One," the older woman said, a little shocked when she realized the two of them had been together all night. But whether it was because he was a human or that hanky-panky in general had gone on in her little sterile kingdom, Chloe couldn't tell.

"Morning," she said cheerfully before resuming her thoughts and her progression upstairs. Maybe there was a whole ceremonial day-after-New-Pride-Leader-speech breakfast fete in her honor. That would be terribly embarrassing, but there might be fruit salad.

Sniffing the air and using her Mai hearing, Chloe was sort of disappointed she didn't hear any of the sounds that might be associated with fete preparations, so she went to the kitchenette instead, where at least she smelled coffee.

Kim was in there already, getting her morning green tea.

"Honored One," she said, dipping her tea bag and her head at the same time.

"Chloe," Chloe corrected grumpily, getting a cup.

Since she had been away, they had installed a cool new coffee machine where you could choose a packet of ten different kinds of coffee, or tea, or even hot chocolate—and press some buttons and the machine would make you almost anything. Of course, the packets were made out of nonbiodegradable Mylar, so as soon as things calmed down around here, Chloe would have to start pushing to get rid of it.

Surely a Chosen One could do that.

Her aim was still a little off: as she poured the milk, the coffee overflowed her cup—at least it wasn't plastic foam—and spilled on the counter.

"Damn," Chloe grumbled, carefully lifting the cup to her mouth to sip the excess off. She almost felt hung over.

"Did you sleep well?" Kim asked.

Chloe frowned, looking her friend in the eye, but there were no double entendres. It was an innocent question.

"Not . . . exactly."

Kim nodded wisely. "Did you and Brian have sex together?"

Chloe choked on her coffee and spat it out, spilling some more from the cup as she did. "What the hell?" she demanded.

The cat-earred girl barely hid her smile. "I was just curious."

Chloe had opened her mouth to say something

about the private lives of Chosen Ones when Igor came into the room.

"Honored One." He gave her a quick nod. "You should come quick. Dmitry is back—he's killed someone."

There goes the happy ending that was just beginning. Why wasn't anything easy?

She followed Igor out and into Sergei's office. Kim came padding quietly behind. For some reason, Chloe didn't mind her constant presence, even when it wasn't exactly invited. She was never distracting, opinionated, or full of herself.

Chloe expected to find him standing tall, impassive, scary, threatening—like he normally was. The kizekh were the soldier class, after all—and from what she had seen at the fight on the Presidio, they were quite effective and disciplined in their own scary, catlike way.

Instead he was sitting on a chair, bent over and weeping. Olga was standing next to him, a hand on his shoulder.

"Honored One!" Dmitry whirled around—of *course* he would have heard them talking. His senses were probably almost as sharp as Kim's. The big guard threw himself to his knees at her feet and touched her ankles. "I did not know! That he was a *murderer* of our people— that he—that he—*killed* our Chosen One!" Chloe was confused for a moment before she realized he meant her biological mother. He was old enough to remember her, she realized, and had maybe even met her before he came over.

"What happened?" Chloe asked as gently as she could, considering there was a crazy murdering adult below her wailing and prostrating himself.

"When I learned the news of our Pri—of Sergei's death, I grew incensed and swore vengeance!"

Chloe turned to glare at Igor.

"He wasn't around when I passed along your no-vengeance thing," he protested. "And even if he was, well, tensions were running a little high. . . ."

"I went to a place where I knew there would be one of the filthy human Order patrolling," Dmitry said, a hard glint in his eye as he recalled. "And killed the coward with my bare claws." Then he began to weep again. "I thought I was avenging our leader, our great protector. . . . I knew you were the One, but he was as a father to us in the days between you and the One before. . . ."

"Do you remember which one you mur—uh, killed?" Chloe asked.

Dmitry shook his head. "They are all alike—brown hair, terrible smell—he was one from the skirmish the other night."

He sounds more Klingon than Mai, Chloe noted.

"You've heard my new rule? No more bloodshed, except in self-defense?" Chloe asked.

"Yes, Honored One. Of course. Our duty is to protect the Pride, not declare war." He looked up at her, his crazy face streaked with tears but set with new resolve.

Chloe wasn't sure if he was asking forgiveness; she wasn't sure that she could have given it. There were more important things to deal with immediately. What was it they said on TV? *Damage control?*

She tried to block out the image of the man before her ripping out the throat of some nameless human, tried to forget that there was a murderer at her feet. *Murder.* Someone's life snuffed out because he was in the path of an angry, vengeful cat person. Not that anyone in the Tenth Blade was exactly innocent, but what if it was someone like Brian? Forced to join, not exactly in complete agreement with the tenets . . .

Chloe went around to Sergei's desk and did the only thing that made any sense—she called Whitney. Directly.

"Hello?" From the obnoxious tone in that one word, she could tell he already knew who was calling.

"Whitney, we need to meet *now*. This is the second death in a week from our stupid little war—we need to end it."

"What second death?"

Chloe looked at Igor and Olga and Kim. They all shrugged—whoever Dmitry had killed, apparently his body hadn't been found yet.

"One of my people killed one of your people in revenge for Sergei's death, against my orders. I don't know who it is, but you might want to issue a roll call."

"Son of a—"

"See? I'm *calling* you to *tell* you about it. I'm being open and honest in an attempt to end this . . . *craziness.*" Amy had a much better word, but somehow Chloe suspected Mr. Whitney H. Rezza didn't know Yiddish.

"If you think I'm going to *thank* you for being the first to let me know about the death of one of my Order or break down weeping and beg for a *truce,* Miss King, especially from *you* . . ."

Chloe wondered if it would have been any different if she had been male. Or older. He only called her "Miss" when he was really upset and looking to insult her.

"Listen. Remember how I asked you about your son?"

"What does—?"

"We have him. *Alive.* Barely."

There was finally silence on the other end. This was a gamble; he seemed more than willing to give Brian up to other members of the Order of the Tenth Blade who thought he had betrayed them by helping Chloe. But Brian *was* his son, after all, and she bet that whatever fate he wanted, it probably didn't involve him ending up at the mercy of the Mai.

"If you want to see him again, *alive,* you will come to"—somewhere public, somewhere safe—"Pier 39, at seven o'clock, with all your little cronies or whatever. This whole thing is ending *today,* one way or another, Mr. Rezza."

She hung up on him again.

It was kind of nice.

She looked up—Olga, Kim, Igor, and Dmitry were all staring at her.

"What?" she demanded.

"You don't, uh"—Igor cleared his throat—"sound like the intern we hired a couple of weeks ago, Honored One."

Chloe just smiled, saving her energy for things greater than laughing.

Seventeen

"I **have never** seen these up close," Kim said, intrigued by the sea lions. She leaned dangerously over the rail, a black baseball cap and her willowy wispiness making her easily mistaken for an overeager young boy.

"You've lived in the Bay Area your *whole life* and you've never seen the sea lions before?" Chloe asked, amazed. Brian tried to stay alert in a wheelchair nearby; Dmitry and Ellen stood guard over him. With his good looks and their weird presence Brian was occasionally mistaken for a celebrity; tourists took candid shots of him, thinking he was *somebody*. Besides this being amusing, Chloe liked having the extra witnesses.

Brian hadn't been completely on board when she told him her plan; he thought it was dangerous for her—and any other Mai involved. But when Chloe asked him what else she could possibly do, he didn't have a better idea.

Amy, Paul, and her mom were with him, too; Chloe

wanted *everyone* who was involved to witness whatever occurred. Alyec pretended to pitch Amy headfirst into the water a couple of times, and Paul even offered to help once. *I'm sure sublimated anger has nothing to do with it,* Chloe thought. Olga was eating a soft-serve ice cream cone, though from her figure it looked like the concept should have been alien. *I wonder if she's also a dairy cat.*

About a half hour after the sun set—it was hard to tell, it being one of those cold gray San Francisco fall days—Whitney strode up with a sleek umbrella he swung like a swagger stick, his expensive raincoat unfurling behind him. There were other people with him, mostly middle-aged, some younger.

"Where is my son?" Whitney demanded immediately.

"I'm right here, Dad." Brian waved weakly.

His father's face went white when he saw the extent of his son's injuries.

"What have you *done* to him . . . ?" Whitney demanded, coming forward, his face now going purple with rage.

Igor stepped easily between him and Brian, arms poised. Ellen and Dmitry loomed forward.

"*We* didn't do anything." Chloe resisted the urge to add, *old man.* "I found him, practically dying, in an alley. *Your* people did this to him."

The old man didn't say anything. He wouldn't deny or confirm it.

"It was Dickless, Dad," Brian said, his thin voice

almost lost in the evening breeze and wails of the sea lions. "He and his little bitches took me by surprise. They left me for dead."

Whitney opened his mouth and closed it again several times. "Richard is dead," he finally said. "The Mai killed him last night."

"Oh," Brian said. "Darn."

"See, this is *exactly* what I mean!" Chloe said, frustrated. "Sergei was killing his own people for power, your people are killing your own people just for—I don't know, old rules. Maybe power as well. And for *what?*" She looked around at everyone gathered there. "What really has been the reason you both have been at each other's throats for so many thousands of years?"

"The Order of the Tenth Blade exists to protect humanity from those stronger who would easily defeat them," Whitney said dramatically.

"Would you take a *look?*" Chloe threw her hand out at her Mai friends. "If your intelligence is *half* as good as ours, you know that there are less than a hundred of us in the West. *A hundred,* Whitney. That's less than the Native Americans, or Tibetans, or Jews, or any *other* dwindling, oppressed minority!"

"Hey," Amy muttered. "I don't think we're dwindling." Paul kicked her to shut up.

"Forget the Tenth Blade: one good earthquake or fire or dirty bomb or terrorist attack and there'd be no more Mai west of the Mississippi. When was the last time, exactly, the Mai actually posed a threat to continued human existence?"

"We have always been there to stop it," Whitney said, drawing himself up. But from the looks on the younger members' faces, he wasn't really convincing anyone.

"And let us not forget the original reason for our existence," a middle-aged woman said, stepping forward. "The villages and cities that were wiped out—"

"Because you raped and murdered one of our sisters!" Igor said, also stepping forward.

"Five. Thousand. Years. Ago. Jesus *Christ,* guys, let it go!" Chloe glared back and forth at both of them. "And may I remind you"—she addressed this to the Order—"the Mai are not *vampires* who prey on the living. You are not vampire slayers who protect the innocent."

"They are fell, foul beasts spawned from the pits," one of the other Tenth Bladers spoke up. "Their existence is anathema to God. Thus they are punished to never have a home and never commingle with true humans."

"You sound like the Rogue," Chloe muttered. "Who, by the way, is an insane psycho killer. And anyway, the whole five-thousand-year-curse thing seems to be over. Brian and I have not only, uh, *kissed* multiple times, but . . ." She didn't want to say it, but if it would further the cause, as it were, well, illusions of her chastity didn't really count much against dead bodies. "Last night, we, uh . . . Look, anyway, the point is, he's *fine.*"

There were shocked looks from everyone, especially Amy. Chloe had *sworn* to her years ago she would be the first to know when It happened. *Technically, it wasn't "It" yet*—she had no desire to get pregnant on top of everything else that was going on in her life right now. But what happened was close enough to It to count.

Brian was blushing furiously, trying to meet his dad's eyes.

"In fact," Chloe said, raising her voice so *everyone* could hear—and hoping she wouldn't be considered a slut, "I made out with *another* human before I ever even met Brian."

"Wait, what?" Brian looked shocked and a little sad.

Chloe ignored him. "And *he's* fine, too. Look, the point is, there is no divine thingy against Mai and humans, uh, loving. We can mix and mingle and mate with no dire consequences."

"The curse seems to have been lifted because we helped save two humans," Kim spoke up, "Chloe's mother and Brian."

Chloe didn't want to meet Alyec's eyes, which were wide with disbelief. No doubt there would be awkwardness and explanations later, even though they were split up.

But her assumption that he was thinking about her was suddenly dashed when Alyec grabbed Amy and kissed her, long and hard. A little too long and hard—Paul and Kim

227

began to look away nervously—but Amy didn't resist. At all.

When they came up for air, Alyec looked her in the face. Amy took a breath, waited a moment, then shrugged. "Nothing. I mean, it was great—but I don't feel weird or anything."

This was not exactly how Chloe had imagined humans and Mai would start to get along better, but hey, it was something. And come to think of it, her usually extroverted friend had been kind of quiet recently. It was only fitting that she steal the spotlight for a moment of silliness during an otherwise deadly encounter.

Edna and Whitney looked appalled, as did other older members of the Order—and Olga and some of the kizekh. Chloe might be mistaken, but some of the other ones looked intrigued. *Not everyone can study sexy cat people without getting a little intrigued.* Opposites attracting and all that.

"The Rogue was just arrested, by the way," Paul interrupted, looking at the news on his phone. "About an hour ago. He's wanted in connection with over a dozen murders. . . . Uh, anywhere else I would say it's the death penalty with the sort of proof they have against him, but I think he's probably going to be committed."

"Welcome to America, lads," Chloe said sweetly to the Tenth Bladers. "And *you* all were born here. This is the way justice happens, not through vigilantes."

"You risk exposing the existence of your own people in doing this," Edna said, but from the baffled look on her face it was obviously a move none of them expected.

"How?" Chloe asked. "You really think that they're going to believe a raving serial murderer when he tells them that all of his victims were actually cats, with claws and slit eyes? Look, I'm still proposing a truce. A *real* truce. You can go on watching to make sure none of the kitties go rabid and start a killing spree, but *no more violence*. If something happens—on either side—it gets dealt with by the police. No more gang wars, no more internecine, uh, necines, and guess what that will mean? *No more innocents gunned down along the way.*" She gave Brian's dad a hard look in the eyes.

"Even if we were to take you up on this 'truce,'" Edna said, covering for Mr. Rezza while he recovered from the remark, "there still remains the little problem of inequity."

"What do you mean? Sergei's dead, Richard's dead, the Rogue will probably go to prison or whatever," Chloe said, thinking furiously. But she came up with nothing. "We're even."

"Not exactly." Brian's dad cleared his throat and spoke up, once again at ease. "There is still the matter of our member who Sergei killed at the Presidio. As far as I can tell, no Mai were even permanently injured in the tussle."

"What do you want *me* to do about it?" Chloe asked

before she could stop herself. As soon as she said it, she knew it was a mistake.

"What Edna said. Equity. The boy Sergei killed and Sergei are dead. But the Mai who killed Richard is still alive. Sacrifice him or her, and we will consider your truce."

Whitney smiled an easy smile of confidence. *I've won*, it said.

"No!" Ellen cried, not with fear, but fierceness. She grabbed Dmitry's arm, her claws extending, her eyes slitting, elongated canines coming out.

As one, the Tenth Bladers stepped back. Chloe could see why just the Mai's existence might terrify some people. Seen this way, they really were kind of like monsters.

"Ellen," Dmitry said calmly, "if this is what the Honored One chooses, this is what must be done."

Chloe panicked. All of her posturing about peace and truce and it had come down to this—a situation she couldn't win. *Leaders sometimes have to make sacrifices they don't like or don't want to, to achieve their goals.* But she couldn't just coldly offer up someone—someone she had watched *Star Wars* with, someone she knew—to die to seal a truce of her making. He even looked willing, as if he was ready to pay for what he had done. Or maybe it was just a look of hopelessness after Sergei's betrayal of the Pride.

With one word, Chloe could send him forward, let the Tenth Bladers kill him, and guarantee a lasting, bloodless future between the Mai and the Order of the Tenth Blade. Wasn't it worth the death of one person?

Yes. But not his.

She *could* offer up someone else, however.

"No, not Dmitry; he was doing what he thought was right at the time." Chloe took a deep breath. "I offer you myself in his place."

Eighteen

A single white gull traced a gentle arc over everyone's heads before heading out over the water. In that one instant, everything was hushed. Then it was over.

"What?" Amy, Brian, and her mom all shrieked at once.

"As the Chosen One, I have nine lives to be given in protection of my Pride," Chloe said slowly. "I think this counts as protecting our future. I offer up one of my lives in the name of 'equity' if this will mean a truce."

It was hard to say who was more shocked—the Tenth Bladers or the Mai. The Mai looked more horrified, the Order of the Tenth Blade more confused.

"I hardly think that's fair," someone from the back of the crowd of the Order called. "It's not really like anyone's going to permanently *die* on their side. . . ."

"Oh, shut up, Carlos," Edna snapped. A pair of tourists walked by, well within hearing range, pointing at the sea lions. "Whitney?"

"The choice is yours, Mr. Rezza," Chloe said quietly. "You can let the killing go on or be remembered as the leader who brought peace to both sides."

"And in a group that has a five-thousand-year memory, that's not too bad," Olga added. "For *both* groups."

That was it. That was key. Blood sacrifice, sure, but ego was everything. Whitney was getting old, and it was obvious Brian wasn't going to follow in his footsteps. The line that had ruled as head of the Order ended with his generation. His second choice, Richard, was dead.

The two tourists didn't seem to notice what was going on as they pushed their way through the Mai and the Order to get closer to the sea lions. The kizekh and soldiers of the Tenth Blade shifted uneasily, but after two bright camera flashes the couple waddled off again, happily oblivious.

"Chloe, don't do this," Brian whispered.

It wasn't like she exactly *wanted* to. Dying twice by mistake and coming back was strange—and, if you really put a lot of thought into it, possibly explainable. Her fall from Coit Tower and survival was a miracle. Being shot in the heart and recovering, well, it was really weird, but not completely unheard of. And her little trips to the Mai afterworld? Low-oxygen-to-the-brain hallucinations.

She didn't have the trust in the Twin Goddesses that Kim had. She only had experience.

Chloe hoped her fear didn't show.

There was a long, tense silence as everyone watched Brian's dad, waiting for his response.

"I think it would be . . . amenable to us, this solution you propose," he said slowly. There was something strange in his face as he looked back and forth between Chloe and Brian. Almost like he realized that his son, brutalized by his own people, was in love with a member of the race he hated.

Guess who's coming to dinner, Chloe thought, trying to bolster her courage.

Whitney gestured to a couple of Tenth Bladers. "Make sure no one . . . comes by and interrupts us." Several military-looking men and women slipped quietly into the thinning crowds that strolled by the pier on the boardwalk.

"Do you really want to do this?" Kim asked, approaching her closely. Not saying no, not encouraging; just making sure. A salty breeze whipped around the two of them, muffling their voices.

"I think," Chloe said, trying to control her breathing, which was a little fast and shallow as her heart beat out of control. "I think the Mai's biggest sin is self-centeredness. Being too self-involved. A little too inward looking, don't you think?"

Kim raised an eyebrow, trying to understand Chloe's crazy thoughts.

"What have we ever done for anyone except ourselves?" Chloe added.

Brian wheeled himself over to her.

"Are you *insane?*" Amy shrieked again, also coming closer. "You don't have to do this."

"I really do," Chloe said, taking her friend's hand.

"It will be by ritual dagger," Whitney said, coming forward. He stopped short when he saw Brian holding Chloe's other hand and the terror in her eyes.

"Can—" Chloe tried to steady her voice. "Can it be Brian?"

Both father and son looked equally surprised.

"I don't see why not," Whitney said finally. "It is . . . it *used* to be a high honor, performing this kind of execution." There were hisses and murmured angry noises from the Mai. "It's only fitting for the son of the head of the Order to do it. But the rest of us will be standing around closely to make sure there are *no tricks.*"

"Wow, Dad. *Thanks,*" Brian said sarcastically.

"Brian, I . . ." His father's eyes traced every injury and bruise and scrape and bandage on his son. "I didn't think they would—"

"*Try to kill me?*" Brian demanded. "What did you *think* Dickless was going to do when you gave him free rein on the 'betrayer'?"

But Chloe was pulled away from the family reunion by Dmitry. "Honored One," he said softly, kneeling on one knee this time, looking her in the eye. "It is my duty—it is my *honor* to die protecting you. Let me do this."

Chloe shook her head, trying to smile but failing. "I'm your leader, and I've chosen. So there it is." *And just one more second of your pleading and I'm gonna wimp out.*

She knelt before Brian in his wheelchair to make it easier for him while pretending to adjust his clothes or something in case the patrolling Tenth Bladers missed some onlookers who might be concerned to see someone's throat being cut. The depths of irony: she was trying to hide her own death.

"I can't do this." Brian shook his head. "You can't ask me to do this."

"It's got to be done," Chloe whispered. "This is the only way to bring peace to the Mai and the Order."

"I can't kill you," he said weakly, a hopeless look in his eyes.

"I can't trust anyone else," Chloe said, kissing his forehead. She tried to ignore the sound of her mother weeping in the background, drowning it out by focusing on the barking sea lions. "I know you'll be careful. Scarring, you know," Chloe added with a smile, although she knew that Brian would understand what she really meant by 'careful'. This was the only way to bring peace, but Chloe couldn't be sure that anyone beside Brian wouldn't slit her throat six more times as soon as she woke back up.

Whitney handed his son the pretty silver dagger. It looked strangely familiar—then Chloe remembered the dream she had where she was her sister and the Rogue cut her down. Same dagger? Or a similar one?

Everyone gathered around them, Whitney the closest, still looking disturbed.

"This is sick," Brian said weakly.

"Hey, I don't trust your old man," Chloe said, her voice shaking. "But I trust you, Brian. I trust you so much."

"I love you, Chloe," Brian said fiercely, a single tear running down his cheek.

"I love you, too," Chloe whispered.

Then he drew the dagger across her throat, and she collapsed to the ground, dead.

Nineteen

When she opened her eyes and saw the strange view of space, the end-of-time galaxies and nebulas spinning above her, Chloe was actually relieved.

It was still a scary place, pitch black with distant echoing roars, on the edge of a cliff with shadows flickering all around, menacing and too close.

But it's better than being dead. Really *dead.*

"Mother?" Chloe asked, getting up and fighting her urge to run. Her voice was lost in the infinitely great space, drowned by the hisses around her like a thousand candles going out. She walked away from the edge of the cliff, toward where the shadows were congregating.

Not that way. Not yet, a voice came to her, growling. A black shadow flame blocked her way. It was both upright and leonine at the same time, majestic and animalistic.

"What do I do now?" Chloe pleaded. "Did I do the right thing?"

You have done the rightest thing our people have witnessed in over five thousand years. Our Pride has never seen a leader like you, not even in me.

"Will we have peace now? Will we be safe?"

For a time—the hearts of both humans and Mai are fickle, Chosen Daughter. You have done the best you can to ensure any peace at all.

"Mother?" Somehow Chloe felt that her time with her mother was coming to a close. "Do you mind me seeing Brian?"

She could have sworn she heard laughter.

Being Mai is a state of mind, a spiritual state as well as that of the body. He loves you, too. What more do you want?

Chloe wasn't sure what kind of answer that was, but her mother didn't seem to be upset by the union.

"Thank you," she said slowly. "I guess I'll be going back now."

Go with my blessings, Chosen Daughter.

There was nothing to embrace, or Chloe would have. The shade of her mother was only fire and air. She turned and faced the edge of the cliff. The winds of a thousand ages blew up it, lifting her hair and stinging her face.

She put her hands out like Superman and jumped.

Twenty

Chloe came to calmly this time, without a jolt or start. *Because I chose to and was ready,* she realized. Her head lay in Brian's lap, sticky with blood. The wound on her neck was already drying up and knitting itself together as she lay there. In a moment, there would only be a faint scar. Like from the bullet. Like from her fall from the tower.

"Chloe!" Brian choked, hugging her as best he could in their two positions.

"That . . . kind of sucked," Chloe said, trying to lighten the mood around them. Then she felt a strange sensation in her stomach. The brave leader and martyr pushed herself off Brian just in time to vomit all over the ground. When her neck pulsed, it *ached* like her worst cramps. One didn't just die and recover immediately; even with Chosen Ones there was suffering in the process. She moaned once, unable to keep it in check.

Dmitry and Amy were at her side, one holding her up, the other holding her hair back.

"Do—do we have a truce now?" Chloe whispered, looking up at Brian's dad. Acid stung her throat.

"We do," the middle-aged man said loudly and authoritatively, but his eyes were suspiciously wet.

Epilogue

This was not exactly how Chloe had imagined attending the fall formal.

For one thing, her dress was kind of last minute—Marisol gave her the choice of one free thing off the racks and Amy had adjusted it for her. Eschewing lace or satin or even cotton, Chloe had opted for a leather bustier and pencil skirt. She felt a little outrageous these days. A red velvet ribbon was tied around her throat as a choker, hiding the scar.

Her date wasn't anyone from her school, and he was in a wheelchair. Brian promised he would try to get up onto crutches for one dance, but Chloe wasn't going to hold him to it. He looked great, actually, very tragic and romantic with his black velvet jacket, pale skin, and luscious dark brown hair. Somehow Amy had managed to scrounge up an antique wheelchair, which helped the image. Brian balked, however, when she suggested a velvet throw over his lap.

Amy was actually dancing with Alyec. They were officially An Item now. And they looked pretty hot together, Chloe had to admit. Her friend was positively gorgeous in the seventeenth-century zombie outfit she had designed.

Paul was sipping spiked punch next to Kim, who didn't bother disguising her ears and eyes; it was a Halloween dance, after all. Everyone complimented her on the "prosthetics." She wore a very prom-y black gown with ruffles and crap, but it actually worked on her, in a sort of otherworldly way.

Paul was still kind of nervous around Kim and Kim was still just drinking in normal human teenage culture; she looked like an orphan suddenly let into a banquet. Somehow Chloe didn't see the two of them hooking up. At least not yet.

"Oh, hey," Brian suddenly said, interrupting her thoughts. "I got you something—I totally forgot."

"*Besides* the corsage?" Chloe teased, fingering the orchids at her wrist. "I'm showered with riches."

As he fumbled in his pockets, she tried to guess what it would be. A little cat figurine? Her name in hieroglyphs, like a cartouche pendant? Catnip?

Instead he pulled out a pin. She squinted at it in the dim light, letting her Mai eyes go slitty for just a moment.

First Woman President, it read, with Wonder Woman standing proudly, hands on her hips.

Chloe laughed. "I think I have all the leadership I can handle right now." She leaned over so he could pin it on. Instead he pulled her forward and kissed her.

"Photo of the charming couple?" Scott Shannon brandished his camera enticingly. There was a portrait area set up in the corner with an actual professional photographer, but he was handling the "action" snapshots.

"That would be wonderful," Kim said excitedly, coming forward and dragging Paul. She beckoned for Amy and Alyec to join them. "Get all of us. I want the tiny ones that fit in a wallet."

"Do you even *have* a wallet?" Paul muttered.

Kim just hissed at him.

Everyone laughed, and the flash went off.

Chloe King has

~~9 Lives~~

8̶

7̶

6

5

4

3

2

1

As many as 1 in 3 Americans
who have HIV...don't know it.

TAKE CONTROL.
KNOW YOUR STATUS.
GET TESTED.

To learn more about HIV testing,
or get a free guide to HIV and
other sexually transmitted diseases:

www.knowhivaids.org
1-866-344-KNOW

Check Your PULSE Book Club

Sign up for the CHECK YOUR PULSE
free teen e-mail book club!

 ⭐ **FEATURING** ⭐

A new book discussion every month

Monthly book giveaways

Chapter excerpts

Book discussions with the authors

Literary horoscopes

Plus YOUR comments!

To sign up go to www.simonsays.com/simonpulse and
don't forget to CHECK YOUR PULSE!

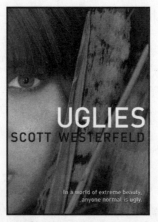

UGLIES

SCOTT WESTERFELD

Everybody gets to be supermodel gorgeous. What could be wrong with that?

In this futuristic world, all children are born "uglies," or freaks. But on their sixteenth birthdays they are given extreme makeovers and turned "pretty." Then their whole lives change. . . .

In a world of extreme beauty,
anyone normal is ugly.

And coming soon: *Pretties*

PUBLISHED BY SIMON PULSE